VIPER'S
DREAM

Critical Acclaim for Jake Lamar

"A fearless young talent to keep your eye on"

—*Entertainment Weekly*

"This one is a gem not just for its plotting but for the extremely likable character of Jenks, who lives in a world of perpetual perplexity where music is the only thing he understands well. Mr. Lamar's love of Paris and his understanding of its ways add to the delight."

—*Washington Times* on *Rendezvous Eighteenth*

"The author casts a tough, critical eye on his cast of mostly black, middle-class, expatriate Americans, whose interactions he so deftly depicts . . . Mainstream readers fond of Paris should feel fully satisfied."

—*Publishers Weekly* on *Rendezvous Eighteenth*

"Always a witty and astute social observer, Jake Lamar illuminates the interaction of French locals with Americans abroad, some of them on the lam, in a suspenseful and funny thriller set in the seamy, particularly fascinating Eighteenth Arrondissement of Paris."

—Diane Johnson, author of *Le Divorce*, *Le Mariage*, and *L'Affaire*, on *Rendezvous Eighteenth*

"A page-turner of a murder mystery with a clear, breezy style. The book is also a wicked black comedy in both senses of the phrase—it's both caustically funny and a shrewd take on racial politics."

—*New York Times Book Review* on *If 6 Were 9*

"Maybe he's feeling the shade of the great Chester Himes, because this novel has wit and sparkle, to say nothing of fabulous characters."

—*Globe and Mail* on *If 6 Were 9*

"Lamar is a skilled tactician . . . The situations and relationships are believable and sharp."

—*Washington Post Book World* on *Close to the Bone*

"Lamar skillfully weaves the romantic with the political, and the personal with the societal."

—*Mademoiselle* on *Close to the Bone*

"A compelling, controversial political thriller, part *A Clockwork Orange,* part *The Manchurian Candidate.*"

—*Kirkus Reviews* on *The Last Integrationist*

"A crackling page-turner . . . Jake Lamar has produced a thriller of ideas . . . A kind of racial *1984.*"

—*Vogue* on *The Last Integrationist*

"A knockout debut. The recollection of a well-to-do African American childhood marred by family discord is as taut as the spryest novel and as revealing as many a hefty sociological tome."

—*Seattle Times* on *Bourgeois Blues*

"On this subject it's a relief to read somebody who doesn't consider it their first task to make you feel at ease."

—*Newsday* on *Bourgeois Blues*

"Dickensian in its power"

—*Atlanta Journal Constitution* on *Bourgeois Blues*

Also available by Jake Lamar

VIPER'S DREAM

A NOVEL

JAKE LAMAR

CROOKED
LANE

NEW YORK

Copyright © 2023 by Jake Lamar

All rights reserved.

Published in the United States by Crooked Lane Books, an imprint of The Quick Brown Fox & Company LLC.

Crooked Lane Books and its logo are trademarks of The Quick Brown Fox & Company LLC.

Library of Congress Catalog-in-Publication data available upon request.

ISBN (trade paperback): 978-1-63910-569-4
ISBN (ebook): 978-1-63910-570-0

Cover design by Gregg Kulick

Printed in the United States.

www.crookedlanebooks.com

Crooked Lane Books
34 West 27th St., 10th Floor
New York, NY 10001

First Edition: September 2023
First published in the UK in 2023 by No Exit Press

10 9 8 7 6 5 4 3 2 1

For Dorli

"It's like an act of murder; you play with intent to commit something."

—Duke Ellington

1

"Tell me, Viper," the baroness asked, "what are your three wishes?"

I am speaking now of November 1961. It was 'round midnight at the Cathouse. There must have been about twenty jazzmen scattered around the place, talking and laughing, drinking and jiving, eating, smoking, toying with their instruments. One could hear the distant plucking of a bass coming from one corner of the house, the errant honk of a saxophone echoing from another, the playful tickling of piano keys. And one could hear a cacophony of meowing, of purring, of hissing, of claws scratching at the furniture. The name *Cathouse* was a double entendre: a home away from home for the two-legged black cats of the jazz world and the actual home of more than a hundred furry felines.

The Cathouse belonged to the Baroness Pannonica de Koenigswarter, "Nica" to her many friends. She was a Rothschild heiress, a blue-blooded European who had parachuted into the New York jazz scene and become a sort of patron, protectress, groupie of the bebop genera-tion. She used to throw all-night party–jam sessions in various luxury Manhattan hotels. It was fun times till Charlie Parker dropped dead in the baroness's suite at the Stanhope. Management was not pleased. That was six years ago. The ensuing scandal made it impossible for Nica to find a place in the city that suited her desire for space and all-night jams. So she bought a Bauhaus-style edifice in Weehawken, New Jersey, just across the bridge from Manhattan, with huge picture windows offering a spectacular view of the glittering metropolis. Thelonious Monk more or less lived at the Cathouse. And the guest list of musicians who passed through, stopped by or stayed a while included the likes of Duke, Satchmo, Dexter, Dizzy, Mingus, Miles, Coltrane . . . I could go on. Lots of folks you've heard of. Plenty more you haven't. This story is about someone you probably haven't heard of. He wasn't a musician but he was as welcome at the Cathouse as any of the jazzmen. Clyde Morton was his actual name. But just about everybody called him The Viper.

You may not have heard of him, but you've most likely seen him in grainy black-and-white photographs going back to the 1930s. He's often there, hovering in the shadows, at jazz clubs, recording sessions, impromptu jams, always deep in the background, dressed in a sharp suit, with a sly smile, pencil-thin moustache, sleek processed hair. You've seen him there at the after-parties, sitting at the far corner of the table, behind the half-empty liquor bottles, the overflowing ashtrays, and plates filled with chicken bones. That look of his. Languid yet dangerous. He sits there, a stillness, a watchfulness about him. There was indeed something reptilian about this man. Everybody was scared of Clyde "The Viper" Morton. Except for maybe the baroness.

"Achoo!"

"Viper, are you allergic?"

"Slightly."

"I never noticed before."

"It's all right, Nica."

"What a surprise. I didn't think you had any weaknesses at all. Are your eyes watering?"

"I'm fine, Nica."

"Viper, are you crying?"

"No, it's just the cats."

"Let me get you a drink. Bourbon on the rocks, yes?"

"Yes."

No, the Viper was no musician. He had wanted to be one. He had the desire. All he lacked was the talent. But he figured if he couldn't make music himself, he'd help those who could by supplying them with some of the inspiration they needed, the elixir of creativity. On this night at the Cathouse, the jazzmen greeted the Viper with the usual gratitude and respect.

"Hey, Viper, how ya doin', my man? Thanks for that last score."

"Viper, you got any of that go-o-o-od shit for me tonight?"

"Yeah, man, I don't know if it was the Californian or the herb from Indochina, but I was so high at that gig at the Vanguard last week—I ain't never played like that. Thank you, Viper!"

Just about everybody at the Cathouse that night was partaking of the Green Lady. The sweet smell of marijuana perfumed the air. And Clyde Morton had provided all of it, if not directly, then through his network of dealers—every ounce, every grain.

"Yo, man, you gonna share that joint or what?"

"Take another hit, then try it in B flat."

"No, no, the way Pops plays it, the trumpet squeeeeeeals at the end. You gotta make it squeal . . ."

The Viper leaned back on Nica's living room couch, languid and watchful, taking in the scene. No one, aside from the baroness, had noticed anything strange about the Viper tonight. But he was indeed fighting back tears. Twenty-five years in this vocation. And until this night, in November 1961, he had killed only two people. Tonight was the Viper's third kill. For the third time in twenty-five years, he had taken a person's life. But this was the first time he had regretted it.

*   *   *

One hour earlier, Clyde Morton stood in a phone booth on Lenox Avenue and dialed the number of his old pal the cop.

"Hello, Detective Carney."

"Viper, is that you?"

"Get a patrol car over to Yolanda's apartment. And an ambulance."

"Is there somebody dead?"

"Yeah."

"I can give you three hours, Viper, no more."

"Thanks, Carney. I guess."

"My advice is: get out of the country. Go to Canada. Or Mexico. Or hop on a plane to Europe. But do it now, Viper. Because in three hours, I'm comin' after you. Three hours. That's all I can give you."

Click. Dial tone.

Viper felt dizzy as he stepped out of the stale, muffled air of the phone booth and into the neon cacophony of

Lenox Avenue. The full force of what had happened, of what he had done, of his crime, his primal sin, seemed to seep into his consciousness, like a drug taking effect. His vision blurred as tears stung his eyes. He had a dreamlike sensation, not of his life flashing before his eyes, but more a feeling of his whole past washing over him. He took in the scene before him, the febrile, sulfurous boulevard he loved. He felt the chill and the drizzle. But still the avenue was bristling with the life of the night. Traffic and chatter. Folks rushed down the street, spilled out of bars and clubs. A restaurant door swung open, and Viper inhaled a mouth-watering aroma, like a gust of spiced wind, smelling sublimely of kitchen grease, of chicken frying crispy in a skillet, of robust barbecue sauce and earthy collard greens. Down-home cookin', folks used to call it. Soul food, in the new argot. Black folks' cuisine. The scent of home. His mama's kitchen in Meachum, Alabama. Relocated to the capital of Black America.

"Black people need to wake up!" Viper glanced at the clean-cut young man standing on a stepladder at the corner, wrapped in a black overcoat, embroidered skullcap on his head, exhorting the passers-by, who ignored him. "America is not ours. This land is not our land. And it will never be our land, even after our ancestors spent three hundred years slaving on it. There is no American Dream for the black man. Wake up from your dream! Recognize that Africa is our Black Motherland! We need to go home—to Mother Africa!"

The Viper couldn't help but smirk, even as he fought back tears. He had been hearing the same speech from the same street corners for a quarter of a century, since the very day he'd arrived here, at the center of the Afro-American universe. Harlem. As he stood on loud, brazen Lenox Avenue, nearly swaying from the shock of what had happened tonight, the night of his third murder, Viper knew this might be the last time he ever saw her, his sweet bitch Harlem.

"We don't even know our history," the smooth-featured young man in the embroidered skullcap shouted as crowds bustled past him in the light, spitty rain. "The black man has lost touch with his past!"

Maybe it was true what the young brother said, Viper thought, even as he felt his own past crashing down on him in waves. Lenox Avenue seemed to swirl.

Haarlem. With two A's. It was Mr. O who first told young Clyde Morton of the original spelling of the place. New York was a tribal town, Mr. O had told Clyde, before he became known as The Viper. The grassy plains of northern Manhattan had been populated first by indigenous Algonquin tribes. In the seventeenth century, Dutch tribes arrived, seized the land and named the region after a city in the Netherlands. It remained mostly farmland until the mid-nineteenth century when tribes of aristocratic white New Yorkers, mostly of British and Protestant descent, built mansions in the countryside, eager to escape the congestion of Lower Manhattan. Equestrians raced horses along rural Harlem Lane. Gentlemen in top hats and ladies holding parasols gathered on the banks of the Harlem River to watch weekend boat parades. Then came the Jewish tribes and rapid urbanization, the construction of row houses and tenements. At the beginning of the twentieth century, the Italian tribes took over Harlem. "Little Italy" was up North before it was recreated in lower Manhattan. Next came the great migration of black people escaping the Deep South. Clyde Morton was one of them. Latino tribes arrived and settled in the east, in what would become known as Spanish Harlem. But as far as Viper Morton was concerned, the true Harlem, the pulsating heart of the place, was black.

"The great Marcus Garvey was right," the young man in the skullcap cried. "We need to go back to Africa!"

Viper was always a bit puzzled by that phrase. How could you go back to someplace you had never been? Detective Red Carney had just urged him to flee to Canada or Mexico or Europe. Maybe, Viper wondered, he should catch a plane to Nairobi.

That was when the baroness pulled up in her silver Bentley.

"Viper, you look so forlorn."

She sat behind the wheel, a cigarette holder clenched between her teeth. Thelonious Monk sat beside her, staring into space, a silk Chinese beanie on his head.

"Maybe I've been waiting for *you*, Nica," the Viper said.

"We're going to my place. Join us."

Viper slid into the backseat. "Hey, Monk."

"What's up, Viper?" the pianist growled.

Everybody knew Monk was the top cat in the Cathouse. On this chilly, drizzly Monday night, still sporting his black silk Chinese beanie, Thelonious sat in an armchair in the corner of Nica's living room. Clearly, he wasn't in the mood for playing the piano. Or for smoking or talking to anybody else. He just sat in the corner, glowering benignly.

The Cathouse was where Viper decided to stay. In another two hours, Red Carney would come looking for him. He would have to be ready. He knew that this night, the night of his third murder, might be the last night of his own life.

"Here's your bourbon, Viper."

"Thanks, Nica."

"May I ask you a question?"

"That depends."

"If you were given three wishes, to be instantly granted, what would they be?"

"Are you messing with me, Baroness?"

"I'm entirely serious. It's my new thing. I ask this question of everyone. Well, everyone interesting. And I write down their answers."

"You write them down?"

"Or you can write them down yourself."

"Why?"

"For posterity, of course. Come on, indulge me. Tell me, Viper, what are your three wishes?"

"Do it, Viper!" The piano player, Sonny Clark, had just sauntered over, high as a kite. "It's fun. Nica asked me last night."

"Yeah, Sonny," Viper said, "and what were your three wishes?"

"One: money. Two: all the bitches in the world. And three: all the Steinways!"

Sonny, Viper, and Nica all laughed.

"All right, Baroness, let me think about it."

"Here's a notepad and a pencil. Play along, Viper. You might be surprised by your own wishes."

Viper decided to take the question seriously. He sat with the notepad and pencil and glass of bourbon on the coffee table in front of him. He pulled out a joint and fired it up. First time he'd gotten high in a year or more. He took a long drag, exhaled slowly. He gave in to the sensation he'd felt on Lenox Avenue. He let himself be carried, swept away, by the waves of the past he felt washing over him. He closed his eyes and imagined he was back there, back home, in Meachum, Alabama, 1936.

*   *   *

"All aboard for New York City!" the conductor hollered.

Clyde Morton had been sitting beside his fiancée, Bertha, on a bench in the Colored Waiting Room of the train station. He rose and grasped his suitcase in one hand, his trumpet case in the other.

"Is you really leavin' me, Clyde?" Bertha said, her voice quivering.

"I ain't leavin' you, Bertha. I'm leavin' Meachum, Alabama. I'm leavin' the South."

"But we got it good here, Clyde. We both got our high school diplomas. We both got good jobs at the cotton mill."

"That ain't enough for me."

"But I love you, Clyde. We engaged to be married. My love ain't enough for you?"

"All aboard for New York City!" the conductor hollered again.

"I got the gift of music, Bertha. Uncle Wilton told me so."

"But, Clyde, your Uncle Wilton is a hobo. He ain't nothin' but a drunk and a thief and a liar!"

"But he sho' can play guitar, you gotta admit it."

"He plays the blues, Clyde. It's the devil's music."

"And I'm gonna play jazz, Bertha. That's even worse, more sinful."

Clyde headed out to the platform. Bertha ran after him.

"But, Clyde, what if you ain't that good, what if you don't make it?"

"I *am* that good. I know I'll make it."

"Don't leave me, Clyde!"

"All aboard! Last call for New York City!"

Bertha was clinging to Clyde now, tearing at his clothes as he strode across the platform toward the train, trying to pull him back into the Colored Waiting Room.

"I gots to go, Bertha! Turn me loose!"

"Don't leave me, Clyde!" she screamed, suddenly hysterical. "Please don't leave me, Clyde! I'll kill myself if you leave me!"

"Lemme go!" Clyde shoved his fiancée, and she fell to her knees.

"I swear to God, I'll kill myself!" Bertha crawled desperately after Clyde, grabbed his leg.

"Damn it, Bertha, let me go!"

Clyde managed to tear away and step up into the train car. The steel door slammed shut behind him. He looked out the window at Bertha, crumpled on the platform, wailing in anguish. "I'll kill myself!"

Clyde heard the chugging of the engine, the screech of the steel wheels on the railroad tracks. As the train pulled away from the station, he looked out the window at his fiancée, still wailing, her voice fading in the distance. "Don't leave me, Clyde! I'll kill myself! I'll kill our—"

The train whistle drowned out Bertha's voice. Clyde hadn't heard the last word she screamed. But he knew what it was.

*   *   *

"Last stop," the conductor cried, "New York City!"

After arriving at Penn Station, Clyde Morton took his first subway ride, hopping aboard the A train. He emerged from underground on a bright, crisp afternoon in September 1936 and stepped into the glory that was Harlem. He was staggered by the noise, the energy, and the sight of all those black folks, black folks from all walks of life: businessmen, businesswomen, mothers pushing baby carriages, street-corner preachers, bums and winos, shady ladies loitering in doorways, proper ladies who looked like schoolteachers, fellas playing dice on the corner—and even a black policeman! He walked around in a daze, his suitcase in one hand, his precious trumpet, in its hard case, tucked under his arm, feeling like a country-ass fool, his eyeballs popping and his mouth hanging open. The biggest city he'd ever seen before was Birmingham, Alabama.

As night fell, he just kept walking around and around, up Lenox Avenue, down Seventh Avenue, and back up Lenox again. He saw with his own eyes places he'd only heard about on the radio: the Apollo Theater, the Savoy Ballroom, Smalls Paradise. And other places he'd never heard of at all but would someday come to know well: the Red Rooster, Gladys's Clam House, Tillie's Chicken Shack. He gaped at the swanky white couples pulling up in their fancy cars for a night of uptown adventure, and black couples, every bit as swanky, striding right past the white folks, without a hint of deference. The colored folks even had an air of superiority, a proprietary attitude. This was Harlem. This was *our* turf.

He checked into a cheap flophouse and lay in his narrow bed, wide awake, listening to the street sounds that seemed to go on all night. He didn't know when he fell asleep, but he woke up, with a start, to daytime noises—trucks and schoolchildren, the sun streaming through the dirty window. It was noon. Clyde went to the corner diner, had a breakfast of ham and eggs and grits, then walked the streets, holding his trumpet under his arm, certain that destiny awaited him. And there it was. He found himself standing in front of a club he had passed by the night before: it was called Mr. O's. And there, written on a standing chalkboard in front of the entrance: "TRUMPET PLAYER WANTED. AUDITION INSIDE."

In a way, he could hardly believe it. But at the same time, he had been expecting just this sort of luck. He entered the club, Mr. O's, filled with an uncanny sense that he was stepping into his future.

"Hello?" Clyde called out. "Anybody here? Hello?"

The club was dark. He could make out the silhouettes of chairs stacked on tables. Suddenly, a light snapped on in what seemed to be the kitchen backstage. More lights flickered on, and Clyde found himself standing in the middle of a dance floor. A big, bearish black man emerged from the hallway. He had a round, jolly face and wore his hat pushed back on his head, the front brim snapped up.

"Hey there, youngblood. I'm Pork Chop Bradley."

"You're Pork Chop Bradley?" Clyde said. "The bass player?"

"You've heard of me?"

"Yes, suh!"

"I've just been hired as the band leader here at Mr. O's. You new in town?"

"Just arrived yesterday, suh."

"Stop callin' me 'sir.' I ain't your daddy or a cop."

"Yes, suh! I mean, okay, sorry, Mr. Pork Chop, I mean, Mr. Bradley."

Pork Chop smiled. He seemed both kindly and bemused. "Where you from, Country?"

"Alabama."

"I'm from Arkansas myself. But I been up here in the big city ten years. Playing in Harlem bands. Is that your dream, Country? To play in a Harlem band?"

"That's my dream."

"How old are you?"

"Nineteen."

"What did you say your name was?"

"I didn't. Sorry. I'm Clyde Morton."

"All right, Clyde. Enough of the niceties. Get that horn out of its case. You know 'Stardust'?"

"I sure do."

"Play it."

Clyde closed his eyes as he played. At first, he felt like he was wrestling with his horn, like it was a giant, slimy, man-sized fish. He was splashing around in the shallow water, trying to haul the beast to shore. Slowly, the flailing stopped. He had subdued the slippery thing. And so he felt in control of his horn. Finally. Yes, he knew Hoagy Carmichael's "Stardust." He knew the Louis Armstrong version, had heard it over and over again on his Uncle Wilton's phonograph. He'd studied it. And standing there, in Mr. O's nightclub, auditioning for Pork Chop, young Clyde Morton played as close to Satchmo as he knew he could ever get.

"Okay, okay, stop," Pork Chop shouted over Clyde's blowing. "Stop right there, son, stop! Stop!"

Clyde lowered the horn from his lips, baffled. "I was just in the middle of the song," he said.

"No, you're done. Clyde, I'm sorry, that was dreadful."

"Huh? What?"

"Is this a practical joke? Did Mr. O send you here as a prank? Is that it?"

"Uh, no, Mr. Pork Chop. I've never met Mr. O."

"Sweet mother of Jesus. You really were auditioning? That really is the way you play? That was the worst shit I ever heard in my life."

"I-I did my best . . . I could try again . . ."

"No, son, there's no point. I mean, I can hear it. Not only are you not a trumpet player, you're not a musician at all. Who told you you were?"

"My Uncle Wilton," Clyde said, his voice cracking. "Down in Alabama."

"I hate to break it to you, son," Pork Chop said softly.

"He's gonna be so disappointed."

"Don't cry, son. You were just dreaming the wrong dream."

"What am I gonna do now?"

Pork Chop gave Clyde a long look, kindly and bemused. "Do you know Mary Warner?" he asked.

"Mary Warner?" Clyde said, swallowing hard, choking back tears. "Who's she?"

Pork Chop chuckled. "Let's go up to the rooftop. I'll introduce you."

Naturally, Clyde had thought Pork Chop was talking about a chick. Some prostitute named Mary Warner. As they climbed the six flights of stairs, he wondered why she would be on the rooftop. But he didn't give it much thought. He was still stunned by Pork Chop's opinion of his talent—or the lack thereof. He knew Pork Chop was right. Clyde had been dreaming the wrong dream. He felt he might swoon when they stepped out onto the rooftop.

He'd never been up so high in his life. The street noise below sounded somehow unreal. He heard pigeons flapping their wings, burbling. But he didn't see any prostitute.

Pork Chop pulled out a cigarette that he'd clearly rolled himself. Clyde watched as Pork Chop lit the cigarette, drew on it with a hissing sound, held the smoke in his lungs, then exhaled slowly. Clyde smelled a sweet yet peppery aroma, unfamiliar but appealing. He suddenly realized: This was reefer. He'd heard of it, yes, but he had never seen or smelled it before. Pork Chop held the cigarette out to him.

"Meet Mary Warner, Clyde. Also known as marijuana. Is this your first time?"

"It is."

"Take a drag, like you just saw me do."

Clyde sucked hard on the joint: *Sssssssss* . . .

Pork Chop said: "Welcome to the fraternity, Mr. Clyde Morton. You ain't no musician, but now you'll know what the jazzmen know. Mary Warner, she was there, in Storyville, New Orleans, when jazz was being born. All the original greats nursed at Mary Warner's teat."

It took a minute, but the effect of the herb gradually kicked in. Now Clyde understood the expression he had heard when folks talked about reefer: getting high. Standing on that rooftop in Harlem, watching the clouds drift by, he felt a dreamy elevation.

Pork Chop said: "Mary Warner is magic. I call it the elixir of creativity."

Clyde took another hit. *Sssssss.*

"Hey, Clyde," Pork Chop said, with a laugh, "you gonna pass that stick back or what?"

Clyde laughed, too, handed Pork Chop back the joint.

When he had walked into Mr. O's nightclub just a little while earlier, Clyde had thought he was meeting his destiny: to be a professional musician. Turned out he was no musician. But he was right about the destiny part.

Pork Chop said: "Vipers. That's what we lovers of herb call ourselves. 'Cause of that hissing sound you make when you take a drag on a joint. I can tell you're a natural born viper, Clyde Morton."

Clyde was soothed by the sound of Pork Chop's voice. There was a serenity about this fat bass player in his battered fedora with the front brim turned up. Pork Chop took another couple of hits on the joint, passed it back to the initiate.

Clyde took a hit. He stared out at the Harlem skyline, hearing Louis Armstrong's sublime rendition of "Stardust" in his head, feeling newly awake, newly alive, tingly and alert. Yet cool, so cool, cool as could be.

"Tell me, Mr. Pork Chop Bradley: Where do you get a hold of this here Mary Warner?"

Pork Chop said: "From the owner of the nightclub. Mr. O himself. Also known as Abraham Orlinsky. I'll introduce you to him someday if you like. I reckon you ain't goin' back to Alabama?"

Sssssss.

"No, Pork Chop. I'm stayin' right here."

"Welcome to Harlem, Viper Clyde."

*   *   *

"If you were given three wishes," the baroness had asked, "to be instantly granted, what would they be?"

November 1961: the night of Clyde "the Viper" Morton's third murder. Viper was stoned. He sat in the

Cathouse, a notebook and pencil in front of him, contemplating Nica's question. He knew that in a couple hours' time, he might be dead or on his way to prison. His pal the cop, Red Carney, had given him three hours to get out of town, to get out of the country. But here he sat, in the Baroness de Koenigswarter's sprawling living room, amid the cats—the jazzmen and the felines—contemplating his three most precious wishes.

"Don't strain too hard, Viper," Nica said. "Write the first three things that come to your mind."

"I'm thinking, Nica," Viper said, a slight edge in his voice. "I'm thinking."

"Yes, of course, Viper," Nica said, suddenly a little nervous. "No pressure at all. Take your time."

The doorbell rang.

"Oh, a new arrival!" the baroness said, cutting a path through a writhing sea of cats, toward the front door.

The Viper was always a little suspicious of Nica. Ever since that night six years ago when Charlie Parker dropped dead in her suite at the Stanhope Hotel. They said it was a heart attack. Bird was thirty-four years old. But the coroner thought he was a man of sixty. That was how much damage he'd done to his body. Yeah, the great Charlie Parker technically died of a heart attack. But everybody knew it was heroin that killed him.

Now this is what you need to know about Clyde "the Viper" Morton. Yes, he was a dealer of marijuana. But he could not abide heroin. He had never used it, and he would never sell it. He forbade anyone who worked for him to sell it. Heroin was a poison. It was the opposite of herb. Marijuana aided the creation of jazz. Heroin was in the process of destroying jazz by killing off its greatest artists.

The Viper didn't know if the Baroness de Koenigswarter had enabled Bird's heroin abuse. But he did know that junk killed Bird, and Bird died in Nica's hotel suite. The Viper had never seen anyone shooting up at the Cathouse. And no one would dare do it in his presence. Everybody knew the Viper was the man to see for marijuana. And everybody knew how he felt about heroin. They knew that if you wanted to deal that shit in the Viper's sphere . . . he would kill you.

"Clyde. Hey, Clyde."

The Viper looked up and saw Pork Chop Bradley standing above him. He must have been the new arrival at the Cathouse. Pork Chop, his friend of twenty-five years. He was still fat, still wore his fedora with the front brim flipped up. But he was an old man now, and he stared down at the Viper with an infinite sorrow in his eyes. He knew what the Viper had done tonight. Knew the person he had killed.

"Hello, Pork Chop."

"Lord have mercy, Clyde. I just came from Yolanda's apartment."

"That's what I figured."

"There was a lot of blood, Clyde. A lot of blood."

Viper said nothing.

Pork Chop said: "How do you feel, man?"

"How do you think I feel?"

"Like you wanna die."

The Viper reignited his joint, took a long hit, exhaled slowly. "I can't die. Not yet." He handed the joint to his friend. "The devil's scared of me. He don't want to meet me face to face. But he knows I'm comin'."

2

C LYDE MORTON HAD NO MEMORY of his daddy. Chester Morton had already been drafted and shipped off to France when Clyde was born in 1917. He didn't lay eyes on baby Clyde till he came home from the so-called war to save democracy. Chester, his wife, and two sons lived in Spooner, Georgia. Chester was a blacksmith. Folks said nobody could shoe a horse like Chester Morton. Before he was drafted, his customers were all black. But after he came home, word spread that Chester was the best damn blacksmith, white or black, in the whole damn county. By the summer of 1919, white customers had started coming his way. That was when Chester Morton's troubles began. One fine morning he received a visit from the chairman of the county's blacksmiths guild.

"You ain't a member of the guild, is you, boy?"

"No, sir," Chester replied. "Guild's all white. Ain't no colored blacksmiths allowed."

"Well, that's exactly my point, boy. You can't be serving white customers if you ain't a member of the guild.

And since you can't be a member of the guild, you can't be serving white customers."

"The white folks come to *me*, mister. They just wants good horseshoes. I can't be turnin' business away. That don't make no sense."

"Don't talk back to me, nigger! Don't think cuz you been to France you ain't still a nigger. You turn those customers away. Or there will be hell to pay!"

The white customers continued to come. Chester Morton continued to shoe their horses. And to take their money. One night, when he was working late at his forge, a mob showed up. They came on horseback. They bore torches and rope, guns and axes and knives. But they were not masked. They felt no need to hide their faces. Clyde would hear years later that his father died hard, cursing his killers till they cut out his tongue.

While the lynching was still happening, a black neighbor showed up at Viola Morton's home with a horse and wagon. He loaded Viola and her two sons and whatever possessions she could quickly gather, and they rode off into the night. By dawn, they had crossed the state line from Georgia into Alabama, and they headed toward Meachum, where Viola's people lived. Clyde Morton was two years old.

* * *

Clyde's brother, Thaddeus, was known to be a good boy. Thoughtful, mature, responsible. Thad and Clyde were home alone one afternoon while their mama was at work cleaning white folks' houses. Clyde was twelve years old at the time, Thaddeus sixteen. Clyde's brother went to the closet and pulled out a hard black case. He opened it.

Clyde felt dazzled by the sight of the shiny brass. He felt as if he were gazing at some holy relic, a talisman.

"Looka here, Clyde. This belonged to Daddy. He brought it home from the war."

"Daddy played the trumpet?"

"I don't think so. He must have found this somewhere in France. Brought it home as a sort of trophy. That night we had to flee Georgia, Mama only had time to pack a few things in the wagon. But she made sure to bring Daddy's trumpet."

"Do you wanna learn to play it?" Clyde asked.

"Nope," Thaddeus said. "Do you?"

"I reckon I'd like to try."

Clyde went to see his Uncle Wilton. He was old. Real old. So old he had been born a slave. Called himself a blues man. He had no wife, no children, no steady job. Made his money playing guitar at juke joints all around the county. His home was little more than a shack. His prize possessions were his guitar, his phonograph, and his collection of blues and jazz records. Or "race records," as they were called back then. Black people's music. Clyde showed Uncle Wilton his Daddy's trumpet.

"You wanna learn how to play, Clyde?"

"Yes, Uncle Wilton."

"Well, the best way to learn to play is to listen. And the best trumpet player in the world is Louis Armstrong."

Uncle Wilton, with a ceremonial air, put a record on the turntable, gingerly dropped the needle.

The first blast of "West End Blues"—the first fifteen seconds of Satchmo's squealing horn—was like a crazy call to arms, an antic reveille, alarming and sublime.

From that day on, Clyde started teaching himself to play, with Satchmo as his model and Uncle Wilton as his guide. Over the next seven years, he worked harder practicing the trumpet than he did studying his school assignments. Mama and Thaddeus warned him about Uncle Wilton.

"Don't waste your time on foolishness with that good-for-nothin' old bum," Thad told Clyde. "Be like me. Get your diploma. Get a decent job. Don't be a disappointment to Mama."

Thaddeus sought respectability. When he was twenty-one, he left Meachum to become a Pullman porter. They were those black men in caps and uniforms who worked on trains all across America. They hauled white folks' luggage, shined their shoes, ironed their clothes, made the beds in the sleeping cars, acted as waiters and cooks. There were black folks who considered Pullman porters important men, role models. To Clyde, they were nothing more than servants. After Thad left to become a traveling butler, Clyde graduated from high school and got a job at the cotton mill. But he still dreamed of being a trumpet player. And his musical mentor encouraged him.

"I hear you play that horn of yours," Uncle Wilton said, "and I know you got the gift. Look at me. I coulda made it. I coulda been a big-time blues man. For me, the dream was Memphis. Maybe Chicago. But I could never find a way to get out of Alabama. Don't let that happen to you, Clyde. You could be the next Louis Armstrong. But you gotta get yourself to New York City. Harlem. That's where jazz be happenin', Clyde. You gotta get the hell out of Meachum, Alabama. You ain't but nineteen years old. Get out. Now. Go play your horn in New York."

"You really think I'm that good, Uncle Wilton?"

"I know it. You could be the next Louis Armstrong. I just know it."

"But I got a good job at the cotton mill."

"Quit it."

"I'm engaged to be married, Uncle Wilton. You met my girl, Bertha."

"Leave her."

"But Uncle Wilton . . ."

"Get out! Now!"

Clyde gathered all the money he'd saved up all his life and bought a one-way ticket for New York the next day. He bolted from the station, from the Colored Waiting Room, suitcase in one hand, his daddy's trumpet in the other, and Bertha hanging all over him, screaming hysterically, then falling to her knees, crawling after him, wailing as the train pulled away from the platform, the screech of the steel wheels and the piercing whistle drowning her out:

"I'll kill myself! I'll kill our—"

* * *

I am speaking now of 1936, Clyde Morton's first full day in Harlem. He'd already auditioned for Pork Chop Bradley and been told he had no talent. Then the burly bass player consoled Clyde by taking him up to the rooftop and introducing him to Mary Warner. After a while they climbed down the stairs, and together they walked the streets of Harlem, high on Mexican locoweed. Clyde's senses felt sharpened. Everything seemed more vivid. He was enchanted by the vibrancy of his people, the varied richness of skin tones. Afro-Americans were often called "colored people" back then, and Clyde felt newly attuned to the beauty of the mix he saw in Harlem, from ebony to mahogany to creamy coffee. He walked with a lightsome spring in his step. Street names floated by: Amsterdam Avenue, 125th Street, St. Nicholas Avenue. He felt keyed in to the soundscape of the different paths Pork Chop led him down: children's peals of laughter, folks greeting each other, joking and jiving, arguing and gossiping on their front stoops, mothers hanging over the rails of iron fire escapes, calling down to their kids playing stickball in the alley. And every few blocks, it seemed, someone was standing on a corner, on a stepladder or a barrel, sermonizing or speechifying: black Christians calling on folks to repent, black Communists calling for a worldwide workers' revolution, black separatists calling for a return to Africa. Clyde took it all in, feeling at once exhilarated and serene. He didn't know where exactly Pork Chop was taking him, but thanks to the Mexican locoweed, he didn't care.

It began to dawn on Clyde that not everyone in Harlem was black. As Pork Chop led him past a huge department store called Braunstein's, Clyde could see through the picture windows that, while all of the clients were black, all of the salespeople were white. He glimpsed the Chinese laundries and restaurants, the Italian bakeries, the Greek diners, the little grocery and big liquor stores with all black customers and all white shopkeepers. Yes, Harlem seemed to belong to *us*, Clyde thought, but who actually owned it?

Pork Chop led Clyde to the famous Gentleman Jack's Barbershop, a Seventh Avenue institution. Now that it was clear he wouldn't be playing in a band, the kid needed some kind of job. Starting with the tinkle of the bell above the door, Clyde felt surrounded by joyful noise, the voices and laughter of black men, of clippers buzzing and scissors snipping. Pork Chop presented him to the boss. Gentleman Jack was elegant and austere. With his caramel skin, pencil-thin moustache and sleek, processed hair, he resembled Duke Ellington, but in an immaculate white barber's tunic.

"You know how to cut hair, Clyde?"

"No, sir, Mr. Jack. But I'd like to learn."

"Well, I ain't got time to teach you now. Can you shine shoes and sweep floors?"

"Yes, sir!"

"You're hired."

"Thank you, Mr. Jack!"

Pork Chop gave him a pat on the back. "Congratulations, Clyde."

"Thank you, Mr. Pork Chop!"

"Big Al," Jack called out. "Get this fella a tunic."

"Why I gots to do it?" a deep voice bellowed.

"'Cause it beats standin' in a breadline, Al! Now get off your ass!"

Gentleman Jack glared at the young employee sprawled in a barber's chair, wearing a white tunic of his own, reading a newspaper. Evidently, he was in a lull between clients. When he rose from the chair, Clyde saw that Big Al was a strapping six and a half feet tall. He gave Clyde a look that said, *I could squash you like a bug.*

"C'mon, Country," Big Al said to Clyde, "I'll get you set up with a locker. And a broom—ha, ha, ha!"

Clyde followed Big Al past the shoeshine stand at the back of the barbershop, down a flight of stairs, and into a basement locker room. Big Al sneered at Clyde as he buttoned up his tunic. He grabbed a broom from the closet and shoved it in Clyde's hands.

"Don't forget—this is the busiest barbershop in Harlem, Country. There's *always* hair to sweep up. Ha ha ha!"

*   *   *

Pork Chop had told Clyde he was dreaming the wrong dream, believing he could be a musician. Now, all Clyde dreamed of was staying in Harlem. During his first two weeks in the capital of Black America, he spent ten hours a day sweeping the floor and shining shoes at the barbershop. Gentleman Jack paid him at the end of each day. And he was earning good tips. Clyde actually loved his job. The shop was a microcosm of Harlem. All manner of black men came through those doors to get their hair cut and, more often than not, straightened, processed, conked. Doctors from Harlem Hospital, lawyers and teachers, preachers and plumbers, mechanics and morticians—they all came to Gentleman Jack's. Clyde was earning enough to pay for his room at the boarding house and to eat out every night. And, best of all, to buy some of Pork Chop's superb reefer.

Pork Chop let Clyde hang out backstage at Mr. O's nightclub. From the wings he watched all the musicians who, unlike him, actually had talent. And afterward, he got to hang out with them at their parties, where there was always booze, women, music . . . and the fragrant herb.

"Mary Warner helps you play better," Pork Chop expounded to a cluster of jazzmen at one lively late-night gathering. "Your senses become more acute. And you relax. You go mellow and get sharp—simultaneously. You feel your instrument in a different way, hear the music inside your head. Mary Warner is magic. The elixir of creativity. That's why it's illegal."

"Pork Chop, quit philosophizin'," said Bill Henry, a clarinet player wearing a natty striped bow tie, "and pass that damn stick!"

Pork Chop was not just the band leader at Mr. O's nightclub; he was also the man to see for Mr. O's Mexican locoweed. He sold little packs of carefully rolled marijuana cigarettes, called 'em sticks: fifty cents for a joint, five dollars for a dozen. Mr. O himself remained something of a mystery. Clyde had been hanging out at Mr. O's club nearly every night for two weeks and had never seen the man.

"Hey, Pork Chop, where your boss been anyway?" a buxom beauty in a polka-dot dress inquired at one of the crowded and smoky late-night post-gig parties. "I miss my sugar daddy!"

"Evening, Estella. I don't know where Mr. O at. Down in Mexico, I reckon. But have you met Viper Clyde here? He's new in town."

"Well, hello, Clyde. Where you from, sweetie?"

"Alabama, ma'am."

"Oh, I didn't know they made men as delicious lookin' as you in Alabama," Estella cooed.

Suddenly a deep voice bellowed: "Hey, Estella, why you wasting your time with that country-ass nigga?" Big Al rose from the couch he'd been lounging on, approached Clyde and Estella menacingly.

"Oh, go shit in your hat, Big Al," Estella said. "Walk me home, Viper Clyde?"

"Yes, ma'am."

Big Al glowered at them as they left the party.

Sometime in the near future, Estella would boast that she gave Clyde Morton "the first pussy he ever got in Harlem."

* * *

"We have a very special client this morning," Gentleman Jack said.

Clyde and his boss were the only people in the barbershop. Gentleman Jack had instructed Clyde to show up at eight o'clock, an hour before opening time.

"Man the shoeshine stand."

"Yes, sir, Mr. Jack," Clyde said.

"I'll be back."

Gentleman Jack disappeared down the stairs to his basement office. Clyde was suddenly nervous. Why would Jack leave him alone when a very special client was about to arrive?

The bell over the door tinkled, and in strode a tall, pale, stork-like white man, long legged with knobby knees, long necked with a throbbing Adam's apple. He wore a dark blue pinstripe suit and a black derby. Clyde guessed from his wrinkled face that the very special client was in his sixties, but he moved with the energy and quickness of a much younger man. And he talked louder and faster than anyone Clyde had ever heard.

"You must be Clyde! Pleasure to meet you. Abraham Orlinsky. Everybody calls me Mr. O. But you know that already, don't you? Let me get up on the big chair here. Thanks for the early shoeshine."

"Thank *you*, sir! It's a—"

"You're from Alabama, correct? First time up North, yes? Have you ever met anyone like me before? Yes, no? I mean, a Jew? Ever meet a Jew before? That's what I figured. Probably never met an I-talian, a Pollack, or a Chinaman either. I'll bet that since you arrived in New York, what is it, two weeks, now? I'll bet you haven't even been outside of Harlem. We'll take care of that today. I can see why people speak so fondly of you. Handsome, polite. A certain rough-hewn charm. Do you box? I'll take that shrug to mean you've never been in the ring before. But I'll bet you've been in a few scraps in your day, haven't you, Clyde? That's what I figured. I'm an investor. That is to say, I dabble in various businesses. A nightclub, as you know. But I'm involved in many endeavors. And as an investor, I can tell you, the most important investment I make is in people. I invest in people. And I have a feeling you just might be a sound investment. Nice shine, Clyde. Thanks. Let's go. You're coming with me today. Oh, don't worry, Gentleman Jack knows all about it. You game? That's what I figured."

Parked in front of Gentleman Jack's barbershop was Mr. O's silver Rolls-Royce, gleaming in the sunshine. Standing beside the car was a chauffeur in cap and livery. He was a short, young black man, barely five and a half feet tall.

"This is my driver, Peewee," Mr. O said. "Say hello to Clyde, Peewee."

"Very pleased to meet ya." The diminutive chauffeur gave Clyde a big grin, but his eyes were wary under the brim of his cap. Peewee opened the door, and with a dreamy sense of unreality, Clyde stepped into the back of the Rolls-Royce.

"Peewee, let's introduce Clyde to Manhattan."

Peewee drove them all around the island. From the back of Mr. O's Rolls, Clyde saw for the first time, with his own eyes, the Empire State Building, the Statue of Liberty, Times Square, Central Park. And the whole time, Mr. O never stopped talking.

"New York is a very tribal city. The tribes are defined by ethnicity. And so are the neighborhoods. You got Chinatown and Little Italy downtown, the Irish in Hell's Kitchen, the Jews on the Lower East Side and the blacks in Harlem. I happen to feel there is a natural affinity between the blacks and the Jews. We were both enslaved, after all. Go down, Moses! Let my people go! God, I love Negro music. That's your people singin' my people's story. Both our people's story. The tragedy in this country is you blacks don't have access to capital. That's why I like to invest in Harlem, invest in black folks. Blacks and Jews. Together, we can do great things in this city."

Throughout the tour, Clyde sometimes glimpsed Peewee spying him in the rearview mirror, the chauffeur's eyes glittering under the brim of his cap.

Clyde wasn't sure how many hours had passed when Mr. O abruptly said, "Peewee, take us to Eddie's gym."

They were back in Harlem. A vast, dark grotto of a gym. The stink of sweat. Men pounding swinging heavy bags, pounding each other, skipping rope, growling and grunting. Mr. O led the way through the crowd of brown bodies, striding in front of Clyde and Peewee. He was the only white man in the gym, but no one seemed fazed by that. At the back of the gym stood a squat, old, bald-headed, light-skinned man with a face that made Clyde think of a bruised piece of fruit.

"Eddie here is the best trainer in Harlem," Mr. O said. "Eddie, meet Clyde Morton. What do you take him for, Eddie, a welterweight?"

Eddie spat on the floor and grumbled, "Middleweight, I'd say."

"Great, let's see him in the ring against one of your sparring partners."

Clyde began to panic. "Mr. O, excuse me, sir, I ain't no boxer."

"I know that, Clyde. I just want to see how you hit."

They put Clyde in trunks and boxing gloves, shoved in a mouthpiece, strapped a leather helmet around his head. Before he knew it, he was in the ring, in a crouch, fists up, facing his opponent, who seemed to be named Crusher. They slowly circled each other, like two big cats, circling and circling. A crowd had gathered around the ring.

"Take him out, Crusher!" someone shouted. "Go get him, man! Show this kid who the boss," someone else yelled. "Damn it, Crusher, hit him already!"

There was no doubt who the crowd was rooting for. Then Clyde saw Peewee, in his cap and uniform, standing close to the ring, right beside an anxious-looking Mr. O. Suddenly, the little driver screamed in his high-pitched voice: "Kick his ass, Clyde!"

Crusher swung at Clyde. Clyde ducked, stepped back and let go a roundhouse right to his opponent's jaw. Crusher went down, out cold.

The crowd erupted in one deafening "Whoooaaa!"

Mr. O grinned and said, "That's what I figured."

An hour later, Clyde was in a cozy fitting room, a tailor named Seymour fussing over him, measuring, snipping, marking the fabric with chalk. This would be the first suit he'd ever owned. Mr. O stood nearby while Peewee sat in a chair in the corner, watching everything.

"All the best tailors in Harlem are Jewish, Clyde. All the best tailors in New York, for that matter. Ain't that right, Seymour?"

"Whatever you say, Abe, whatever you say," Seymour muttered. "This *schwartze* is not as big as the last one you brought me."

"You ready to talk business, Seymour?"

"Step into my office, Abe."

The two old men disappeared, and Peewee and Clyde were suddenly alone in the fitting room.

"How ya doin', Clyde?"

"All right, I guess. I just don't know what your boss wants from me."

"He's grooming you."

"Yeah, but for what?"

"You'll see."

Mr. O and Clyde returned to Gentleman Jack's barbershop at seven thirty that evening, half an hour after closing time. Gentleman Jack and his top deputy, Carlton, were waiting for them. Big Al was sweeping the floor.

"Thanks for staying open late for us, Gentleman Jack."

"My pleasure, Mr. Orlinsky. Big Al, you can go home now."

Big Al set down the broom and glowered at Clyde as he stalked out of the shop.

"I'd like you to give Clyde a conk, a shave, and a manicure," Mr. O said. "Make him look almost as good as you, Jack."

"Have a seat, Clyde."

"I ain't never had my hair straightened before," Clyde said.

"Nothin' to it," Jack said.

Yeah, right. Clyde screamed when the sizzling lye hit his scalp.

"Aaaarrrrgggh!"

Gentleman Jack, Carlton, and Mr. O all had a good laugh. "First time's the worst time," Jack said. Clyde's scalp was still burning as Jack combed out the naps.

The whole time Mr. O stood by the barber's chair, observing the process.

"So here's my proposition, Clyde," he said. "I'd like you to be my shadow, my body man. Where I go, you go. By day, we'll make business rounds; by night, we'll have a good time. Work hard, play hard, that's my motto."

The bell over the shop door tinkled.

"Here's Peewee with your new suit, tailored shirt, and matching tie. I also bought you some new shoes. We can discuss your salary in more detail later, but for now, here's a one-hundred-dollar advance."

Clyde damn near fell out of the barber's chair when Mr. O laid the five twenty-dollar bills on the counter.

"Get a good night's sleep, Clyde. We'll pick you up at your boarding house tomorrow morning at ten o'clock sharp."

"Yes, sir! Thank you, Mr. O! Thank you!"

The next morning, Peewee drove Mr. O and Clyde back to the tailor's shop. Clyde was wearing the gray pinstripe suit that had been made especially for him. Mr. O led him into the office of the tailor who had fussed over him just the day before.

"Seymour, I hope you've had a change of heart since yesterday."

"Heart schmart, Abe, I told you I don't have the money."

"Clyde, grab Seymour by the throat."

Clyde did as he was told.

"Ach, I can't breathe!"

"Seymour, yesterday I saw Clyde knock a big buck unconscious with a single blow. If he punches you in the face at one hundred percent of his strength, he'll kill ya."

"Lemme go, lemme go!"

"The money, Seymour. One thousand clams. Now."

"I haven't got!"

"Clyde, applying twenty percent of your strength, punch Seymour in the face."

Clyde did as he was told.

"AAAACCCCCHHH!"

Seymour fell to the floor, his face a bloody mess.

"Hit him again, Clyde," Mr. O said.

"No, please," Seymour cried, "please, no!"

Seymour crawled on his hands and knees to a file cabinet in the corner. He opened a drawer, reached way in the back, pulled out a wad of bills, then he crawled back across the floor, held out the money, sprinkled with the blood dripping from his face.

"Here it is. Please, just don't hit me again."

Clyde felt exhilarated. Powerful. Never in his life had he punched a white man in the face. If this was the job Mr. O wanted him for . . . he could get used to this. In some small but significant way, at long last, Clyde Morton had avenged his daddy's death.

CHAPTER

3

I AM SPEAKING NOW OF November 1961. The night of
Clyde Morton's third murder. Pork Chop Bradley had
located the Viper at the Cathouse.

"Achooo!"

"God bless you, Clyde," Pork Chop said.

"Nica and her damn cats," Viper muttered.

Pork Chop and the Viper sat beside each other on the
couch in the baroness's vast living room, passing a joint
back and forth.

"There was a lot of blood, Clyde," Pork Chop said
again, slowly. "A lot of blood."

"Did you see Red Carney?"

"Yeah, but he didn't see me. There was a crowd at
Yolanda's place. Cops. Doctors. Scumbag reporters."

"Carney gave me three hours to disappear. That was
an hour and a half ago."

"So what the fuck are you doing?"

"Well, I've got this notepad and pencil here in front of
me, and I'm contemplating. Nica asked me, if I was given
three wishes, to be instantly granted, what would they be?"

Pork Chop seemed puzzled. "Yeah . . .?"

"So, I'm thinking . . ."

"Are you serious?"

"She's never asked you?"

"Fuck no."

"She's making an archive of responses. She probably didn't think you were interesting enough."

"The baroness already knows my three wishes: music, reefer, and more reefer. It ain't so complicated. You gotta *reflect*? And you wanna do this *now*?"

"What else am I gonna do?"

"Run!"

"That's what I figured you'd say."

"Clyde, listen. You've got to—"

"That's what I figured. Did you hear me when I said that? Who does that sound like?"

"Jesus, Clyde."

"Mr. O. You don't like to talk about Mr. O, do you, Pork Chop?"

"No, Clyde, I don't."

"That's what I figured."

*   *   *

"Gage," Mr. O said. "Reefer. Weed. Pot. Herb. Tea. Muggles. Grass. The Green Lady. The tasty green. Mary Warner. Mary Jane. Only sex organs have more monikers than marijuana."

I am speaking now of 1938. Clyde Morton had been working for Abraham Orlinsky for two years. He was twenty-one years old, had his own apartment on Lenox Avenue, wore custom-tailored suits, and was gettin' laid. And every night he got high on Mr. O's Mexican locoweed. One sultry summer evening, riding in the back of the Rolls-Royce, the boss fired up a joint, took a long drag, then handed the spliff to his body man. The chauffeur, Peewee, watched them warily in the rearview mirror.

"So, tell me, Clyde," Mr. O asked, "which do you think is preferable: to be loved or to be feared?"

They were driving up to Harlem after a long day of meetings downtown. Clyde knew they still had one more business call to make. He was surprised that Mr. O was lighting up before the workday was done. But he followed the boss's lead and took a hit on the stick. Mr. O continued talking before Clyde had time to consider his question.

"As a leader, I mean. A prince or a president or a boss. Ever heard of Machiavelli, Florentine philosopher? Sixteenth century. He posed the question: Is it more important for a leader to be loved or feared? What do you say, Clyde?"

"Both," Clyde said.

Mr. O grinned. "Machiavelli says it's best to be both. That's what every leader wants. But it rarely happens. Almost never."

Years later, Clyde Morton would consider this the happiest time of his life. He hadn't started selling locoweed himself yet. He hadn't met Yolanda. He hadn't killed anyone. Sometimes, back in those days, he felt his main job was listening to Mr. O.

"You're a very clever young man, Clyde. I see leadership potential in you. But clever as you may be, Clyde, almost no leader gets to be both feared and loved. Machiavelli said that you had to choose one or the other. So which one would you choose, Clyde?"

"I don't know."

"That's what I figured."

Abraham Orlinsky called himself an investor. Others called him a dope dealer, a slumlord, a gangster, a pimp, a murderer, a loan shark. He loaned money to men running small businesses, at exorbitant interest rates. And when you claimed you couldn't make your payments, well, that was when Mr. O showed up with Clyde in tow.

Peewee parked the Rolls in front of a liquor store on Eighth Avenue. Clyde followed Mr. O into the store. He didn't know this one, didn't recognize the paunchy, middle-aged white man behind the counter.

"Hello, Max," Mr. O said. "I told you that next time I came by, I'd bring along some muscle."

Max flashed a terrified smile. "Abe, now, c'mon. I've been hearing about this dusky young associate of yours. He looks like a nice enough boy. You and I know that no violence is necessary. We can work something out. I'm—"

"Max, I've supported this enterprise of yours for a long time. I've loaned to you at far lower interests than I've charged other clients. Because I like you. And because I like you, I've been as patient as Job."

"I'm tellin' you, Abe. You're asking too much. I can't run a business this way. It's like I'm trying to function with one arm tied behind my back!"

"Well how 'bout we see if that actually makes a difference?"

"Now, Abe, I'm sure we can work something—"

"Clyde," Mr. O said, "break Max's left arm."

Clyde walked behind the counter.

"No, no, wait," Max said, panicked. "Please—"

"Sorry, mister," Clyde said as he came up behind Max.

Clyde had gotten quite good at this maneuver, knowing exactly how to grasp the limb, how to snap it quickly, how to brace himself for the agonized scream that always followed the hideous crack of the bone.

"Aaaarrrrgggghhh!"

"Now pay up, Max," Mr. O said. "Before you've got *both* arms twisted behind your back."

As Clyde's reputation grew, the need for violent enforcement diminished. After two years, Clyde's day largely consisted of sitting outside closed office doors and eavesdropping while Mr. O cut deals with his clients inside. When it came to enforcement, Mr. O never asked Clyde to hurt a black man. That's because Mr. O never loaned money to black men. He just owned their businesses outright. Take the barbershop: it may have had Gentleman Jack's name on it but full ownership belonged to Mr. O.

At night, Clyde accompanied the boss as he made his rounds of Harlem's swingingest clubs: the Savoy Ballroom, Smalls Paradise, the Club Hot-Cha, and of course Mr. O's very own night spot, bearing his nickname, where Pork Chop Bradley led the house band. On a typical night, Mr. O was accompanied by three or four women. They crowded with him and Clyde in the back of the Rolls. Peewee drove them from one venue to another. Clyde never saw Mr. O with a white woman. All the women he took out were black. Every single one. Every night, he was surrounded by brown-skinned beauties. He always went home with one of them. Which meant that, most nights, Peewee and Clyde benefitted from the company of the women who didn't get picked. And on nights when Mr. O stayed at home, Peewee and Clyde hung out with Pork Chop and other musicians at parties after their gigs, where folks laughed and drank and flirted and danced amid thick clouds of marijuana smoke.

It was at one such party that a fella folks called West Indian Charlie sidled over to Clyde, holding the fattest joint he'd ever seen.

"Hey, Viper Clyde," Charlie said in his lilting accent. "You still smokin' Mr. O's Mexican locoweed?"

"Hell, yes," Clyde said. "And it's still gettin' me high."

Charlie was a taxi driver. And he had recently started peddling some kind of dope from the islands.

"Take a toke on this, my friend. Then—hold on to your hat!"

Sssssssssss . . .

While Clyde sucked on the joint, Peewee walked over.

"Hey, West Indian Charlie, that's some fragrant shit you got there."

"Good evening, Peewee."

"Hey, Viper, lemme get a hit."

As Clyde exhaled and passed the joint, the high kicked him in the head. "Damn, Charlie."

"Potent, is it not?" Charlie smiled. His skin was dark and leathery, and he sported a neatly trimmed goatee. "Caribbean grass is much stronger than the Mexican shit you're dealing for Mr. O."

Peewee sucked on the joint. *Sssssss . . .*

"I don't deal reefer, Charlie," Clyde said. "I'm not in on that part of Mr. O's business."

"Ah, but you will be, Viper Clyde, you will be."

"Hey, man," Peewee said, "this dope is tasty, too."

"Hey, Charlie," a voice bellowed. "I thought I told you not to show up at any party I was at." Big Al came lumbering through the crowd.

"Well, good evening, Big Al. Would you like to try some of my herb?"

"Fuck you and your voodoo shit. I told you I don't like Jamaicans."

"And as I've told you before," West Indian Charlie said in his most musical accent, "I'm not Jamaican, Big Al. As for voodoo, well . . ."

"Relax, Al," Peewee said. "Smoke some of this shit and unwind."

The towering barber loomed over the diminutive chauffeur. "Who the fuck is talking to you, midget?"

"Midget? I'll kick your ass, motherfucker!"

"Kick my ass? Ha ha ha ha ha!"

Now, keep in mind, Big Al was about a foot taller than Peewee. But that put Peewee at just the right level to punch Big Al in the balls.

"Ouf!" Big Al's booming laugh turned into a smothered howl.

As he doubled over, Peewee punched him in the throat. Big Al hit the floor, a felled tree. He writhed in pain, struggling to breathe. Peewee grabbed a beer bottle, smashed it against a table, then straddled Big Al's chest. He held the broken bottle inches from Big Al's face.

"What you got to say now, nigga?" he screamed in his high-pitched voice. The music stopped. Partygoers froze in place, stared at the tiny driver, straddling the giant's chest, ready to plunge the jagged glass into his face. "What you got to say now!" Peewee squealed.

Pork Chop rushed in out of nowhere and pulled Peewee off Big Al. "Stop, Peewee! You'll kill him!"

Pork Chop hustled Peewee toward the door. Big Al lay on the floor, still writhing, struggling to breathe. The music and the dancing resumed.

"Your little friend shows a lot of spirit," West Indian Charlie said.

"Thanks for the smoke, Charlie. I'm going home."

"Let's do business together, Viper Clyde."

"Good night, Charlie."

* * *

Early one morning, Clyde received his first summons to the penthouse. Mr. O phoned and told Clyde to come straightaway to his luxury building on Park Avenue and Eighty-Second Street. Clyde had seen the elegant facade of the building, from the back of Mr. O's car, many times. But this would be the first time he actually stepped inside.

The doorman, a middle-aged black man, greeted Clyde as if he already knew him. "Good morning, Mr. Morton. Please take the elevator on the left side of the lobby."

The elevator operator, another middle-aged black man, was just as welcoming. "Good morning, sir. Here to see Mr. Orlinsky? Yes, sir, I'll take you straight to the top!"

An exuberant, uniformed maid swung open the front door of the penthouse and beamed. "Well, hello, Clyde Morton!" She was plump and cinnamon skinned, about the same age, Clyde reckoned, as his mama back in Meachum, Alabama. "I'm Matilda. Come on in! I've heard so much about you, child! Mr. O is crazy about you, son!"

Clyde tried not to gawk as Matilda led him through the palatial apartment, down high-ceilinged marble corridors decorated with Greek columns. She opened a set of double doors. The smell of marijuana was overpowering. They passed through the room, where four other black women in maid's uniforms sat around a large wooden table. Each of them had a stack of rolling paper and a little pile of joints at her side. And at the center of the table was a mountain of Mexican locoweed. The four maids were chattering away as their fingers rolled joint after joint with expert dexterity. These were the sticks that Pork Chop and other of Mr. O's dealers sold for fifty cents per joint or five dollars for a packet of a dozen.

"Hey, girls," Matilda said as they passed through the room, "say hi to Clyde Morton."

"Hi, Clyde!" the maids called out in near unison. They smiled and glanced at him, but their fingers never stopped rolling.

"Hello, ladies," Clyde said, trying to sound casual.

"Right this way, Clyde," Matilda said, leading him into a book-lined den. It was a small room, dimly lit, intimate.

"Wait here, Clyde. Mr. O will be with you shortly."

Matilda left him alone in the den. There were doors on three sides of the room, all closed. There was a couch and a couple of chairs, shelves filled with leather-bound tomes, and a small reading table, on which lay a copy of *The Prince* by Niccolo Machiavelli. Clyde felt a strange hush. He started flipping through the pages of the Machiavelli. He did not hear a door open. But quite suddenly, he felt another presence in the room. He turned. And there she was.

"Hey, killer."

She was the most radiant person Clyde had ever seen. Skin the color of honey, emerald eyes. She seemed to be lit from within. Even wearing a maid's uniform, there was something regal about her.

"Why do you call me that?" he asked.

"Just something about you."

"My name is Clyde."

"I'm Yolanda. My friends call me Yo-Yo. But you ain't my friend. Yet."

"How old are you, Yolanda?"

"I'm almost eighteen."

"From your accent, I'm gonna guess you're from New Orleans."

"You have a good ear. Are you a musician?"

"I wanted to be a trumpet player. But I had no talent."

"I'm gonna be a singer. I want to go on stage at Amateur Night at the Apollo, but Matilda says she won't let me until I'm twenty-one!"

"Matilda. The head maid?"

"She's my aunt. She's looking after me. I got kicked out of Catholic school in New Orleans a couple of months ago. My parents sent me up here as punishment. But they know I ain't gonna spend my life being no maid!"

"No, Yolanda. You're a star. Anyone can see that."

"Are you making fun of me?"

"No. I'm not. You're a star."

"I was born to sing. Did you ever think you were born to do something?"

"Right now, I'm thinkin' I was born to meet you."

"You *are* making fun of me."

"No. I am entirely serious."

"He's coming! Bye, killer."

Yolanda scooted out one door as Mr. O opened another.

"Step into my office, Clyde."

"Mornin', Mr. O."

Mr. O's office was so spacious and airy, its bookshelves so towering and tidy that it reminded Clyde of the 135th Street branch of the New York Public Library (a place he'd visited often after hearing his boss speak of different works he must read).

"Have a seat, Clyde. Let me get straight to the point. Have you ever heard of Adam Smith? British economist. He said the basis of capitalism is supply and demand. That's how I made a fortune during Prohibition. There was gonna be a demand for liquor no matter what the law said. So I supplied. Now, it seems there is a growing demand for marijuana. Ten years ago it was something only the musicians knew about. Now, people who come to hear the musicians wanna get high, too. White folks comin' up to Harlem are hankering for it. So I'm expanding my supply of Mexican locoweed and modifying the means of distribution. From now on, distribution will be centralized at Gentleman Jack's barbershop. It will be run out of a former basement storeroom that has been nicely refurbished as an office. And you will be the executive in charge of distribution and sales."

"Does that mean I won't be your body man anymore?"

"That's what it means, Clyde. Your official title will be business manager at Gentleman Jack's. The Mexican loco-weed will come to you. But you won't see any Mexicans. Peewee will bring you a satchel full of joints each Monday. You will distribute the twelve-joint packets to a network of dealers who will come by your office every week to stock up and to deliver the previous week's earnings. They will seem like ordinary barbershop customers, and I will be able to launder the profits through that very legitimate enterprise. Peewee, after dropping off his satchel of joints each week, will return from your office with a satchel full of cash. I will carve up the earnings. Everyone will get a nice cut. But especially you, Clyde. I will also have you personally dealing herb to our preferred clients. This is a major promotion, Clyde. Reefer could end up being a very big business. But it could also be very, very dangerous. So, are you in?"

"Of course, I am, Mr. O."

"That's what I figured."

*   *   *

And so began the vocation that would make Clyde Morton's name. To Harlem's vipers in the know, he became *the* Viper. The business out of Gentleman Jack's basement exploded in the first three months of operation. It happened so fast, Clyde got a little anxious. He shared his worries with Peewee during one of the chauffeur's drop-offs at the barbershop basement office.

"Here you go, Clyde," Peewee said, placing a satchel full of joints on the desk. "This week's supply."

"And here are the fruits of last week's demand," Clyde said, placing an identical satchel, but one filled with cash, on the desk.

"Life is beautiful."

"Lemme ask you, Peewee. You don't ever worry that some of the dealers are holding out, do you?"

"Holdin' out on *you*, Viper?"

"Yeah."

"Not a chance, man. It's like Mr. O says: in Harlem, you are both loved and feared."

"I am?"

"Damn straight. White merchants fear you 'cause you've done them serious bodily harm with impunity. Black folks love you for that very same reason. But black folks also fear you. All your dealers is black. They figure if you can assault white folks and get away with it, you'd be even more brutal with one of your own people. They wouldn't dare hold out on you."

"Have you been reading Machiavelli?"

"Who he?"

* * *

Clyde "the Viper" Morton had just stepped out of Gentleman Jack's one evening, when a stocky white guy in a shabby suit walked right up to him. His face was flush and freckled. Two uniformed cops trailed close behind him. He flashed his badge.

"Detective Red Carney, New York Police Department."

And with that introduction, right there in front of all the black folks on loud, proud Seventh Avenue, Red Carney punched Viper in the face.

"Up against the wall, nigger!" Carney screamed. "Search him, officers. Empty his pockets."

"What the fuck is this all about?" Viper yelled, feeling his mouth fill with blood from his burst lip.

"Shut the fuck up, nigger!" A crowd started to gather. "Back away, you people," Carney barked. "Back away."

"I ain't scared of you," Viper said as one of the uniformed cops roughly frisked him.

"Oh, you ain't? Well, you oughta be!" Carney said. He gut-punched Viper, who promptly collapsed to the sidewalk, gasping for air. "I'm takin' your black ass to jail. Put him in the car, officers."

At the station, the cops threw Viper into the cell so violently, his head banged against the wall and he blacked out. When he came to, it was early morning. Two cops pulled him off the cot in his cell, dragged him down a hallway into a small, nondescript office, and plopped him down on a metal chair. His head throbbed. He saw the freckle-faced young cop sitting across the metal desk in front of him.

"Morning, Viper," Red Carney said, sounding almost friendly. "Jeesh, your face is a mess. Sorry about that, but it had to be done. And we had to make a public show of it. I'm covering for Mr. O in this little business you're running out of the barbershop. You don't know it yet, but I'm gonna be the best ally you'll ever have."

"Can I go now?" Viper said.

"Of course," Carney replied. "Mr. O's waiting for you."

The silver Rolls-Royce was parked right outside the station. Peewee sat behind the wheel, eyeing Viper warily from under the brim of his chauffeur's cap as he slid into the back seat, beside Abraham Orlinsky.

"Good morning, Clyde. Rough night, eh? Sorry, but this had to happen. Red Carney has to look like he's on to anything you might be up to."

"I understand, Mr. O," Viper said.

"That's what I figured."

"But I don't have to like it."

"No, you do not. Take the day off, Clyde. Peewee?"

"Yes, sir?"

"Let's drive Clyde back to his place."

*   *   *

As Peewee pulled up in front of his Lenox Avenue brownstone, Viper didn't recognize the figure standing at the foot of the stoop. He registered that it was a black man in a dark blue cap and uniform but only as he stepped out of the Rolls-Royce did he realize it was a Pullman porter: his older brother, glaring at him, his face twisted in disgust.

"Sweet mother of Jesus," the porter growled.

"Hello, Thaddeus."

"Look at you, Clyde. What evil have you got yourself mixed up in?"

"Nice to see you, too, brother. What has it been, two years?"

"Two and a half."

"Lemme buy you a cup of coffee."

Viper led his brother to a diner down the street. The head waitress gasped at the sight of his battered face. "Take the booth in the corner, Viper," she said. "I'm gonna bring you a cold compress for that eye, too."

"Thank you, sweetheart."

The brothers settled into the booth. They sat in silence until the waitress brought the coffees and the ice pack. Finally, Thaddeus said, "Two and a half years, and not a word to our mother."

"I didn't know what to say, Thad. I left home to become a musician and learned at my first audition that I had no talent. I was ashamed."

"Because you listened to that damn fool Uncle Wilton."

"How is he?"

"He's gone blind. Syphilis. Lost his mind, too. He's locked up in the state hospital."

"I'm sorry, Thad. I'm sorry I was so stupid. I was no musician. But I'm making something of myself now. How is Mama?"

"Heartbroken. Because we've heard about you, Clyde. *I've* heard about you. The Pullman porters are a nation-wide network. We're riding trains all over this country. And certain folks get talked about. My little brother Clyde is much talked about. First, I heard you were the shake-down gorilla for some Jew gangster. Now I hear that you're dealing drugs! And you say you're making something of yourself?"

"Do you know how much I earn in a week, Thaddeus? A lot more than you make as a traveling butler."

"You're proud of yourself?"

"Hell yes, I am! And next year, I'll have enough money to go back to Meachum and buy Mama a house!"

"Mama don't wanna see you, Clyde! That's what I come here to tell you. Don't nobody back home wanna see you. Not after what happened to Bertha."

"What?"

"You really didn't know. Your fiancée, Bertha, remember her?"

"Damn it, Thad."

"You left her cryin' at the train station."

"How is she doin'?"

"You really don't know."

"Know what?"

"Bertha killed herself."

"She what?"

"Six months after you disappeared without a trace. Nobody knew where you were or what had happened to you. Bertha slit her throat with a straight razor."

"No! Oh, no!"

"Bertha was pregnant. I suppose you didn't know that either."

"I . . . I . . . I suspected."

"Nine months pregnant when she slit her own throat."

"And . . . and . . . the baby?"

"What do you think? What do you care?"

"Thad, I'm, I'm so sorry."

"I'm leaving." Thaddeus rose from his seat, straightened his cap, tugged on the lapels of his uniform. "I've got a train to catch. I just came here to tell you one thing, Clyde: don't ever go back to Alabama."

* * *

"Tell me, Viper," the baroness had asked, *"what are your three wishes?"*

At the Cathouse, in Weehawken, New Jersey, in November 1961, Pork Chop Bradley tried to talk sense to his friend.

"Clyde, I think you're in a state of shock. From what happened at Yolanda's tonight. But you have got to pull yourself together."

"Leave me alone, Pork Chop. I'm thinking."

Pork Chop shook his head in exasperation. "Suit yourself."

The bass player rose from the couch and walked away, through the thicket of cats, to the other side of the baroness's vast living room.

Viper picked up the notepad and pencil. Suddenly, it had come to him. He scribbled his first wish:

I wish I'd never left home.

4

LATE NOVEMBER 1940. WAR HAD broken out in Europe. President Franklin D. Roosevelt had just been elected to a third term in office. And Viper Morton was a prince of Harlem. He cruised the capital of Black America in his big black Cadillac. The pimps and prostitutes in the five-block stretch known as The Market; the illustrious doctors and attorneys, politicians and entrepreneurs who lived in the exquisite townhouses of Strivers' Row, those two blocks of prime Harlem real estate; the musicians, the singers and dancers, the artists and writers, the children of the Harlem Renaissance who strutted their stuff along Lenox Avenue: wherever Viper Morton steered his luxury automobile, folks knew who he was. Older men tipped their hats as he glided by. Some women blew kisses. Men his age—the Viper was all of twenty-three at the time—stared in awe and envy. Folks called out to him:

"Hey, Viper! Lookin' good, my man . . ."

"How ya doin', Viper? I'll see you tomorrow at the barbershop."

"Viper, baby, you said you was gonna come to my birth-day party!"

"Hey, Viper, I'm dancin' at the Savoy tonight. Come backstage and say hi after the show."

The reefer business was booming. The office in the basement of Gentleman Jack's barbershop was the perfect center of distribution for Mexican locoweed. Viper's deal-ers fanned out across Harlem. And thanks to Detective Red Carney's protection, the cops left Viper alone. Some of the men in blue even gave a respectful nod when passing Viper on the street.

When Viper Morton showed up at the Apollo The-ater, he was given the best seat in the house. When he turned up at the Red Rooster for his favorite dinner of barbecued spare ribs and cornbread, management always found a table for him, no matter how crowded the res-taurant was. When Viper walked into Braunstein's depart-ment store, where the customers were all black and the sales people all white, Arthur Braunstein Jr., son of the late founder, waited on Viper himself. Viper liked dropping by the jewelry counter, picking out baubles for his latest short-term girlfriend. Or adding to his collection of flashy wristwatches. Recently, he'd treated himself to a pair of diamond-studded cufflinks shaped like horseshoes—in honor of his father. Best of all, Viper never even had to pay.

"I'll add it to your line of credit, Mr. Morton," Arthur Braunstein Jr. always said with a wink.

Mr. O had been right when he told Viper two years earlier that white folks were gettin' hip to the Green Lady. He had Viper handle the most prestigious clients person-ally, usually from a corner table in the nightclub. And one of his most frequent customers was Arthur Braunstein Jr.

"Ah, Viper, you should have been here in the Roaring Twenties." Arthur would sigh wistfully over his dry Martini, after slipping his dealer five bucks for a pack of a dozen joints. Braunstein Jr. was still in the prime of life, not yet fifty-years-old, but like so many of Mr. O's longtime buddies, he pined for Harlem's past, waxing nostalgic about the old Cotton Club, forgetting perhaps that, back in the day, Viper would only have been allowed to be employed, not seated, at the famed Harlem establishment where the entertainers and the servers were all black and the customers all white.

"I met Scott and Zelda there," Arthur Braunstein Jr. would say just about every time he visited Viper's nightclub table. "Ah, the speakeasies, the gin joints! You don't know what you missed."

"I was a barefoot boy in Alabama back then."

"Ah, yes," Braunstein Jr. would sigh. "I envy your youth." Then he'd knock back the last drops of his Martini and say, "Give Mr. O my regards."

"I certainly will."

In actual fact, Viper didn't see Mr. O all that much anymore. The boss man had rarely ventured up to Harlem in the past year. Most of their transactions were through Peewee, chauffeur and bagman for large sums of money and vast quantities of herb.

Viper had been summoned to Mr. O's Park Avenue penthouse a total of three times to discuss business. That first time was when he laid eyes on Yolanda.

My friends call me Yo-Yo. But you ain't my friend. Yet.

Viper didn't see Yolanda at all the next two occasions. He had only seen her that one time, in Mr. O's small, book-lined den, two years earlier. But he thought

of Yolanda nearly every day. And he dreamed about her
at night.

* * *

Weekends, naturally, were always the peak time for reefer
sales. And for many of the hippest folks in Harlem, the
weekend only ended at four o'clock Monday morning, with
the breakfast party at Hutch's Hideaway. Hutch's wasn't
really a nightclub, yet wasn't really a restaurant or diner.
Located in a basement on 133rd Street, it was only open
five hours per week. Every Monday, from four AM till nine,
Leroy Hutcherson served up pancakes dripping in maple
syrup with fat slabs of bacon, heaps of eggs, and steam-
ing grits while bands played and folks ate and danced and
flirted away the waning hours of the weekend before stag-
gering out into the Monday morning glare. Viper's dealers
always sold a lot of Mexican locoweed at Hutch's place.
And Mr. O had wangled a special deal with Red Carney.
Hutch's Monday breakfast was one of the few public places
where folks felt free to fire up a joint. Viper was used to
catching a whiff of Mexican locoweed amid the aromas
of downhome cookin'. But on this particular Monday as
he walked into the hoppin' scene at Hutch's Hideaway, he
smelled something funny. Familiar yet unusual. Herbal,
yes, but more fragrant and spicy. It was that Caribbean
dope.

"Well, hello, Viper, come join me."

West Indian Charlie was sitting alone, finishing off a
plate of pancakes.

He looked prosperous in a sharp suit and a pair of gold
cufflinks Viper had eyed at the Braunstein's jewelry counter. "Good to see you, my friend. Please, sit."

"Hello, Charlie. First time I've ever seen you in here."

"Yes, and it won't be the last. You smell my herb, don't you? I saw you sniff the air when you came in the door."

"I noticed it," Viper said evenly.

"I understand full well, Viper, that Mr. O has been the only dealer selling to this establishment for some time. But I think Hutch is happy to have a little variety on the menu."

"Charlie, we have been content to have you peddling your Caribbean herb but . . ."

"You don't want me selling on your turf. Well, this is precisely what I wanted to discuss with you, Viper. I am selling a product that is superior to your locoweed, and you know it. We should join forces."

"You and me?"

"Not just us," Charlie said, his accent taking on an even more musical lilt. "We should form an independent black dealership. I have more supply channels from the islands opening up. I've got connections at the Port Authority. And my taxi stand is the perfect money-laundering operation."

"So what do you need me for?"

"Viper, are you kidding me? Prestige, business acumen, police protection."

"I would lose Red Carney's protection the minute I left Mr. O."

"Not necessarily. Think about it, Viper. With me in charge of supply, you and Peewee handling distribution and sales, and Big Al providing us with the muscle—"

"Big Al?"

"Yes, I've approached him as well. But you and me and Peewee. It would be the three of us, three proud black men, running a business together. This is the moment for us to seize control of the reefer market in Harlem. Before the Italians come in. Gage is still something strange to the Mafia. Now is the moment for us to take over, Viper. The only thing standing in our way is Mr. O. An old white man."

"Welcome to America, West Indian Charlie," Viper said with a chuckle.

"You laugh, but on the island I come from, the slaves rebelled. We didn't wait for the white man to give us our freedom. We took it. I'm inviting you to now take your freedom from Mr. O."

"In your West Indian revolt, the slaves killed their masters?"

"Exactly."

West Indian Charlie looked vaguely devilish with his leathery skin and pointy goatee. Viper took his eyes from Charlie's gaze, tilted his head ever so slightly. That was when he suddenly saw her, sitting in a booth in the far corner of Hutch's Hideaway. Yolanda. With her honey skin and emerald eyes. Yo-Yo. But he was not allowed to call her that. Not yet. He saw her, in her purple party girl dress, take a slow drag on a joint, exhale dreamily, then stub the stick out in the ashtray. She must have sensed his gaze. Their eyes met. She broke into a sunburst of a smile. Viper's heart soared. At just that moment, Peewee walked up to Yolanda's table. He was in civilian clothes, not his chauffeur's uniform. The little man saw Yolanda looking at Viper. He turned to his friend and business partner and smirked. The gloating expression on his face said, "Yeah, man, that's right—she's with *me*!" It was five in the morning. Had they been out all night together? Peewee took

Yolanda by the hand and led her through the crowd, out of the breakfast club.

"Well if it ain't my two favorite niggas!" A familiar cackle broke the Viper's concentration. "Viper Clyde and West Indian Charlie!"

"Good morning, Estella," Charlie said.

"Hey, baby," Viper said. "How you been?"

Estella plopped down in Viper's lap. He hadn't seen her in a year or more. She'd aged startlingly. Estella was only about thirty years old, but her face was haggard, her eyes hollow.

"Don't you, 'hey, baby' me, Clyde. I saw how you were oglin' that high yellow bitch. Let me make you forget all about her."

"Looks like you two know each other," West Indian Charlie said.

"Know each other? I gave this country boy the first pussy he ever got in Harlem! Ain't that right, Viper Clyde?"

"Well, uh, Estella, I . . ."

"You got something for me, Charlie? I ain't got no money on me but—"

"No worries, Estella. I'll add it to your tab."

Charlie reached into his jacket pocket. Viper expected him to pull out a joint, but instead he handed Estella a little square of wax paper.

"God bless you, West Indian Charlie."

Now Viper understood. Charlie wasn't just dealin' his Caribbean herb. He was pushing heroin.

"Well, I'm off." Charlie rose from the table. "I'll let you two get reacquainted. And, Viper, think about what we discussed."

"Sure, Charlie."

"C'mon, Viper, baby," Estella cooed. "I'll make you forget that high yellow bitch. Let's get outta here."

"And where are we gonna go?"

"To paradise."

*   *   *

Out on the street it was still nighttime dark. Estella led Viper down to one of the seedier stretches of Eighth Avenue. Aside from the occasional bum, curled up and sleeping in a doorway, there was no one on the street. A few delivery trucks rolled by. Estella turned down a side street and pushed open the front door of a decrepit tenement. The building seemed half abandoned. Doorless doorways gaped open to reveal dark and empty apartments. Viper smelled urine in the stairwell. A rat scuttled across the third-floor landing. They climbed to the fourth floor. Estella cracked open a rickety door.

"Wake up, you good-for-nothin' niggers!" she cackled.

There were six men scattered about the room, slumped in armchairs or on the sofa. Viper recognized them all. They were musicians. Most of them either stared into space or were nodding off. Viper felt like he had just walked into the waiting room for hell. Only one of the junkies was playing his instrument: Bill Henry sat in the corner, fumbling with his clarinet, his trademark striped bow tie knotted tidily.

"Hey, Viper, what you doin' here?"

"Hello, Bill."

"You got the shit, Estella?"

"Damn right, Slim."

Slim Jackson, a gifted sax player, was slumped on the couch, looking sickly, barefoot, wearing nothing but baggy pants and a dirty undershirt. Slim squinted and only now seemed to recognize the man standing in front of him.

"You bought the shit from the Viper?"

"Hell no, Slim," Viper said. "I don't mess with smack."

"Aw, Viper, man, you should try it."

"Here, Slim. I got the shit from West Indian Charlie."

This was the first time Viper had been in a shooting gallery. He sat down and fired up a joint. He watched Slim Jackson hunch over a wooden crate that served as a sort of coffee table, preparing the heroin, mixing it with liquid in a metal spoon, heating up the spoon with the flame of his cigarette lighter. Viper shuddered at the sight of the needle. Slim strapped a belt around his arm, pulled it tight, stuck the needle in his bulging vein. His eyes rolled back in his head.

"Aw, damn, that's sweet."

"C'mon, Slim," Estella cried. "Do me up, baby!"

"I'll help you, Estella," Bill Henry said. He set down his clarinet and shuffled over, took the needle and belt from Slim, grasped Estella by the arm. Gently injected her.

"God bless you, Bill."

"Sure you won't give it a try, Viper?"

"You go ahead, Bill. I can't stand needles."

"I got what you want, Viper," Estella said. "Come with me."

Estella led Viper down a hallway, into a dark, threadbare bedroom. The air smelled of stale sweat, like a locker room. But Viper didn't care. He was horny. And he was still thinking of Yolanda. Estella stretched out on the bed.

"Come here, baby," Estella said. "I'll make you forget that high yellow bitch."

They didn't even get out of their clothes. Viper dropped his pants around his ankles. Estella lifted her skirt and pulled down her panties. The entire act lasted only a few minutes, and as soon as it was over, Viper fell asleep.

Later, he would have no idea how long he lay unconscious beside Estella. It was the smell that woke him. A putrid, syrupy stink. Before he opened his eyes, he felt the sticky vomit on his cheek.

"Aaaaarrrrrgggggh!"

He jumped backward off the bed, fell against the wall. Estella lay on her back, on the bed, her eyes wide open, lifeless, a stream of syrupy puke streaming from her mouth—Hutch's Monday breakfast—spreading across the pillow.

Viper stumbled down the hall, found the bathroom. Leaning over the rusty sink, he washed Estella's vomit from his face. When he returned to the living room, all the junkies were asleep. Except for bow-tied Bill Henry. He continued to fumble with his clarinet. He looked up at Viper, his eyes glazed.

"Hey, Viper. What you doin' here?"

"Goodbye, Bill."

Viper left the shooting gallery. Daylight had broken. The streets of Harlem were starting to buzz. He returned to his apartment on Lenox Avenue, cracked open a bottle of bourbon. He drank until he passed out. He had a vision of Bertha, his fiancée, back in Meachum, Alabama. She stood naked in a bathroom, in front of a mirror. Her belly was swollen. Nine months pregnant. She held a straight razor to her throat, her hand quavering violently. Then, just as she drew the blade across her neck—

* * *

The rattling telephone jolted him awake.

"Hello?"

"Hello, Clyde."

"Hello, Mr. O."

"Come see me at the penthouse. Right away."

Viper drove downtown.

"Good afternoon, Mr. Morton."

The black doorman of Mr. O's building was, as always, full of bonhomie. So was the black elevator operator.

"Well, hello, Mr. Morton. I'll take you straight to the top!"

Matilda, the head maid, was as plump and jolly as ever as she swung open the front door.

"Well, look at you, Clyde Morton. More handsome every time I lay eyes on you!"

And the maids busily rolling joints greeted him in singsong unison . . .

"Hi, Clyyyyyde."

. . . as he and Matilda passed through the sunny, joint-rolling room.

For his part, Viper tried to hide how shaken he still felt by what had happened at the shooting gallery that morning.

"Mr. O will be with you shortly."

Matilda left Viper alone in the small, book-lined den with doors on three sides. *The Prince* by Machiavelli lay in its place on the reading table. Suddenly, the honey-skinned, emerald-eyed girl slipped in through one of the doors, dressed in her maid's uniform, as silent and agile as a cat.

"Hello, killer."

"Quit calling me that, Yolanda."

"Why? It suits you. I'm sorry we didn't have a chance to talk this morning, at Hutch's Hideaway."

"You were with your boyfriend."

"Peewee's not my boyfriend. I've never even let him kiss me."

"Then what were you doing out with him at five in the morning?"

"I'm a prisoner in this penthouse! Aunt Matilda watches me like a warden. But she goes to sleep early, especially on Sunday nights. So, once in a while I sneak out with Peewee. He takes me to clubs and makes sure that I'm home before Matilda wakes up at six o'clock."

"This is a regular thing of yours? Sneaking out with Peewee Sunday night?"

"It's happened three or four times. I get to listen to bands, learn my craft."

"And Peewee does this out of the kindness of his heart? Doesn't even expect you to give him a kiss?"

"He says he wants to marry me."

"So you're leading him on?"

"I am under Matilda's control until I turn twenty-one. That's thirteen months from now. Only then will I be free. I'm gonna walk out of this place and become a singer, a great jazz singer."

"And what about Peewee?"

"Damn it, Clyde, don't you understand? It's you I want!"

"No, Yolanda. I didn't understand that."

Yolanda stared hard into his eyes. She walked right up to him, stood so close their bodies were almost touching.

"You can call me Yo-Yo now."

She spun around and quickly, silently slipped out the same door she had entered through. Two seconds later, the door on the other side of the den opened.

"Come on in, Clyde," Mr. O said.

"Your call sounded urgent."

Viper was startled by the sight of Mr. O wearing a dark velvet bathrobe over silk pajamas. This was the first time he'd ever seen his boss in anything but a business suit. Mr. O seemed weak as he shuffled in his slippers toward his desk. They sat across from each other in Mr. O's spacious and airy library of an office. Viper had never seen his boss so subdued, solemn.

"I heard about Estella," Mr. O said. Only then did Viper see that the old man's eyes were red-rimmed. He had been crying. "How she died."

"News travels fast."

"I have ears everywhere, Clyde. I've known Harlem longer than you've been alive. I remember Estella when she first arrived from South Carolina. Just as cute as could be. And so excited to have made it up North." The old man paused, and his Adam's apple trembled in his long, pale throat. "Now, they're sending her body back down South for burial. All because she had the bad luck to meet West Indian Charlie."

"He's a businessman."

"Heroin is a filthy business, Clyde. I would never deal that poison, would you?"

"Not after what I saw this morning."

"What sort of animal pushes junk?"

"Charlie has approached Peewee and me."

"And Big Al. Yes, I've heard. I tried out Big Al as my body man before you came along. He's a cretin."

"Decent barber, though."

"And West Indian Charlie is some kind of voodoo witch doctor, you know that, don't you?"

"I don't believe in that stuff."

"You realize what Charlie's real plan is, don't you? He wants you to rub me out, so that he can then rub you out. He wants our entire business. To replace Mexican loco-weed with his Jamaican gold or whatever the hell they call it. Charlie would have all of us dead. You must see that, don't you, Clyde?"

"Yes, I do."

"We need to put West Indian Charlie out of business. Permanently. And you have to be the one to do it, Clyde. Peewee will be your accomplice. But you have to be the one who does the deed. You knew this day would come. When you would have to go to the next level. Are you ready to do that, Clyde?"

"Yes, Mr. O, I am."

"That's what I figured."

Mr. O had already worked out a meticulous plan for how the deed would be done. But he left it up to Viper to sell the scheme to Peewee. Viper saw this as Mr. O's test of his leadership, his Machiavellian moxie.

*   *   *

Early the next morning, Viper met the little chauffeur on the rooftop of Mr. O's nightclub, the same place Pork Chop had taken young Clyde Morton to smoke his first joint four years earlier. It was sunny but bitingly cold. Pigeons warbled. A seagull screeched overhead. Six stories below, horns honked and traffic zipped along the avenue.

Viper could have begun with small talk, maybe asking Peewee about his date at Hutch's Hideaway Monday
morning. He wondered if maybe Peewee would be the one
to bring up Yolanda, to boast of his secret Sunday night
outings with his would-be fiancée. But Viper didn't give
him the chance. He got straight to business: "Mr. O has
an assignment for us."

"Damn," Peewee said after Viper made his pitch.
"Mr. O done thought through every detail. How much he
gonna pay us?"

"Ten grand each."

Peewee whistled. "Shouldn't you get more?"

"If we get caught, they will send your black ass to the
electric chair along with mine. Same risk, same pay."

Peewee nodded. "And Red Carney's on board?"

"Yes," Viper said. "I met with him last night."

Peewee paused. He removed his chauffeur's cap,
scratched his head, put the cap back on, and stroked his
chin. Finally, he asked: "Any reservations?"

"Only one," Viper said. "Somehow, this doesn't seem
fair. West Indian Charlie is selling a product that's superior
to ours."

"All the more reason to take it off the market," Peewee said. "Besides, you're just talkin' herb. Charlie's dealin'
heroin. We gotta get that shit outta Harlem."

"So, you're in?"

"Let's kill the motherfucker."

*   *   *

That night, at half past eleven, Viper and Peewee entered
Gentleman Jack's barbershop through a back entrance that
gave out on a dark alley. The front door had been locked,

the street side windows shuttered since closing time at seven PM. They waited in the main room, with its wall-sized mirrors and plush barber chairs. Viper had approached Big Al at his barber's station that afternoon, telling him to go see West Indian Charlie at the taxi stand, to tell him they had a deal and to arrange a midnight sit-down. At the stroke of midnight, Viper and Peewee heard a key in the front door of the shop. The little bell above the door tinkled, and in walked Big Al and West Indian Charlie.

"My comrades!" Charlie exclaimed, vigorously shaking hands with Viper and Peewee. "I am so pleased about your decision." He handed Viper a briefcase. "Ten thousand dollars. Consider it a signing bonus."

"We ain't signing shit, Charlie," Peewee said. "But we'll take your money."

"Count it if you like."

"There'll be time for that," Viper said. "Listen, Big Al—Peewee, Charlie and I need to discuss business details that don't concern you. I'd like you to go back to your apartment. Take this briefcase. I don't wanna leave all that cash here. We'll come by your place when we're done here."

Big Al looked perplexed. He stood stock still, blinking rapidly. Viper turned to Charlie, raised his eyebrows inquisitively, posing the silent question: *You with me on this?*

"That's fine by me," Charlie said.

"I thought I was gonna be a partner," Big Al bellowed.

"Shut the fuck up, Al," Peewee said in his needling, high-pitched voice. "You the muscle. And you should feel lucky to have that damn job since everybody seen me kick your ass. You remember that time, Al, with the bottle?"

"That's enough, Peewee," Viper said. "Go on home, Big Al."

"Don't even think about stealin' our money," Peewee said. "And lock the door to the barbershop on your way out. We don't want nobody wandering in here thinking they can get a midnight conk."

"Anything else?" Big Al asked, glowering.

"You excused," Peewee said.

Big Al, briefcase full of cash in hand, lumbered out of the shop, locked the door behind him.

"Charlie," Viper said, "take a seat in Big Al's chair. This is his barber's station. How about a drink? We've got Jamaican rum."

"That sounds fine," Charlie said. "But, you know, I'm not Jamaican."

"Peewee, three shots, if you please."

The chauffeur took out a bottle and three glasses from a cupboard.

"Shame about Estella, huh, Charlie?" Viper said.

"Ah, Viper, one can't afford to be sentimental in our line of work."

"I guess you're right."

Peewee handed shot glasses brimming with rum to Viper and Charlie. "Gentlemen," Viper said grandly, raising his glass. "To our success!"

The three of them clinked glasses.

As Charlie leaned his head back and swallowed his shot, Peewee slid behind him, pulled a pair of handcuffs out of his jacket. As Charlie lowered his arm with the shot glass, Peewee grabbed his wrist, cuffed him to the brass arm rail of the barber's chair.

"What the fuck!"

Viper grabbed Charlie's free arm. Peewee took out a second pair of handcuffs, chained Charlie's other wrist to the rail of the big barber's chair.

"You treacherous motherfuckers!" Charlie screamed, writhing helplessly, both wrists chained to the chair, kicking at the air. "Don't you know what I am? If you harm me, you will be cursed till the end of your days!"

Viper lifted a straight razor from Big Al's barber's station. He grabbed Charlie by the hair, jerked his head back with one hand and, with the other, held the blade to his throat.

West Indian Charlie started growling, muttering incoherently. It sounded like furious gibberish.

"Ade Due Damballa. Secoise entienne mais pois de morte."

Viper's hand was quavering wildly, the blade an inch from Charlie's throat.

"Cut him, Clyde!" Peewee squealed.

Charlie muttered furiously.

"Morteisma lieu de voucuier de mieu vochette."

"What's he sayin'?" Viper asked, struggling not to panic.

"Some voodoo shit!" Peewee cried. "Kill him!"

"Endonline pour de boisette damballa!"

Viper slashed. Blood exploded in a geyser, splattered the huge mirrors.

"Damn!" Peewee cried.

Charlie fell limp in the barber's chair, making a grotesque gargling sound. Blood streamed from his slit throat, soaking his shirt front.

Viper and Peewee moved briskly, according to plan. Viper dropped the razor. Peewee undid the handcuffs.

Passed them to Viper, who pocketed them. Days later he would return them to the man who had loaned them to him: Detective Red Carney.

Viper and Peewee went to the basement bathroom. Washed the fresh bloodstains from their clothes and hands. Exited through the back entrance, into the dark alley. They went to Mr. O's nightclub, soon found themselves at a table with a bevy of brown-skinned beauties from Brooklyn, come up to Harlem for a good time. At about one o'clock, the rumors started. There had been a murder at Gentleman Jack's.

By one thirty, the cops arrived at Big Al's apartment.

"Open up, Al! This is Detective Red Carney of the New York Police Department!"

They banged on the door while Big Al cowered behind his couch. Finally they knocked the door down. It took four uniformed cops to hold down the flailing giant and cuff his hands behind his back.

"Alvin Oakley," Carney snarled, "you are under arrest for the murder of Charles Louis Delambert, alias West Indian Charlie."

"It was the Viper!" Big Al screamed, exploding in violent sobs. "You all know the Viper did it, you motherfuckers!"

"Sorry, Big Al," Carney said. "This is an open-and-shut case."

The papers were full of it the next day. A dozen witnesses on Seventh Avenue had seen Big Al entering Gentleman Jack's at midnight with West Indian Charlie, who was carrying a briefcase. A little while later, Big Al was seen leaving alone, locking up the barbershop, said briefcase in hand. Charlie had been killed at Big Al's barber's station, his throat slashed with Big Al's razor. And Big Al was found with Charlie's briefcase and the ten thousand dollars inside it. Presumably, he was getting ready to flee to Mexico that very night—before the cops burst in.

Two days after his arrest, Big Al hung himself in his cell.

*   *   *

Something changed after that. Clyde "the Viper" Morton still cruised the streets of Harlem in his big black Cadillac. But folks no longer called out to him. The older men didn't tip their hats. The women stopped blowing kisses. Now, folks tended to look away, with a sort of shy deference. There was no more love for the Viper among his people. There was only fear.

5

Nobody is sure of the exact date, but it was some-time in 1961 that the Baroness Pannonica de Koenigswarter started posing the question to jazz musicians at the Cathouse: "If you were given three wishes, to be instantly granted, what would they be?"

Many of them wished for mastery over their art. Just as many wished for money. Some wished for world peace. Nica's favorite response had come from Thelonious Monk.

> *One: To be successful musically.*
> *Two: To have a happy family.*
> *Three: To have a crazy friend like you!*

Nica had never seen anyone dwell on the question as long and as contemplatively as Viper Morton on this November night. He sat on the couch, staring into space, with a strange air of concentration. He was as still as a snake sunning itself on a rock. A pencil was poised between his fingers. He had scribbled something on the notepad in front of him, but from where Nica stood, she couldn't read the words. Something was wrong with The Viper. Nica saw it right away when she and Monk pulled up to the corner in her Bentley as the reefer man stepped out of the phone booth on Lenox Avenue. Pork Chop Bradley had arrived at the Cathouse a half hour ago. He and Viper had a tense exchange, but Nica hadn't been able to hear what they had said to each other. Now Pork Chop sat in a corner, fingering his bass and occasionally casting anxious glances at the Viper, who remained oblivious, lost in thought.

Viper was the first non-musician to whom Nica had asked the question. Was that why he took so long to consider his answers? Or was it because he was a gangster and was cautious about what he put down on paper?

Nica decided to bring her guest a fresh bourbon on the rocks. He turned his head slowly toward her as Nica set the glass down on the coffee table; she studiously avoided a glance at what her guest had scribbled on the notepad.

"Here you are, Viper."

"Thank you, Nica."

"You know, I usually photograph the people I ask about their three wishes. But you wouldn't like that, Viper, would you?"

"Are you secretly working for the FBI, Nica?" Viper asked with just the faintest trace of a smile.

The baroness let go a fluty laugh. "Surely, you're joking! J. Edgar Hoover has been trying to have me deported for the past six years!"

The doorbell rang.

"Pardon me."

Viper knew the FBI was said to have been trying to send the baroness back to Europe—ever since the night Charlie Parker had dropped dead in her hotel suite. Yet he was still suspicious of the way she had just suddenly materialized in the jazz world, getting to know all these musicians, spreading around all this money, this hospitality. What was in it for the baroness?

"Well, look who's here!" Nica trilled as she swung open the front door of the Cathouse.

"Hello, Baroness," Viper heard the famous gravelly voice answer.

In walked Miles Davis. Coolest motherfucker on the planet. Wearing pitch-black shades in the middle of the night. At this moment in time, Miles was king. Viper worried about him, though. A few years ago, Miles had had a ferocious heroin habit. Finally, he'd locked himself up in his Daddy's house in East St. Louis, gone cold turkey. It was Charlie Parker who had turned Miles on to junk. Miles was playing in Bird's band, and everybody wanted to emulate Bird. They figured to play like him, you had to shoot up like him. Now, with Bird six years dead and Miles's own career thriving, Viper could only hope the trumpeter was staying away from junk. Miles sauntered over to him. Viper reached into his jacket pocket and pulled out a plump joint.

"Thanks, Viper," Miles growled.

"Anytime, Miles."

"What you writing, your memoirs?"

"Nica asked me my three wishes. I'm contemplating."

"Yeah, she asked me the same question a few weeks ago. I told her I had only one wish."

"What was that?"

"To be white!"

Miles exploded in contemptuous laughter.

*   *   *

"Yesterday, December 7th, 1941," the president intoned, "a date which will live in infamy—the United States of America was suddenly and deliberately attacked by naval and air forces of the Empire of Japan."

It was midday, and Viper listened to FDR's address on the radio in his basement office at Gentleman Jack's. This was the same office that Detective Red Carney had decided *not* to search that night—one year earlier—when they framed Big Al for West Indian Charlie's murder. After the speech, Viper was listening to the congressional vote to declare war when Peewee walked glumly into his office in his cap and uniform. He plopped down in a chair. Viper clicked off the radio. He thought the little man was saddened by the sudden outbreak of war. But no.

"It's over," Peewee said.

"What is?"

"Yolanda and me."

"Matilda's niece?"

"Don't act like you didn't know, Viper. We were engaged to be married. She just called it off."

"Why?"

"Today's her twenty-first birthday. She is now officially out of Matilda's control. And she told me she liked me, but she wasn't gonna marry no chauffeur."

"Damn, Peewee, I'm sorry."

"I told her I ain't just a chauffeur. I'm a businessman! And I ain't gonna be drivin' Mr. O around forever."

"What did she say to that?"

"She just laughed in my face. Like I'm so pathetic. Bitch think she white."

"She's New Orleans Creole."

"Which means she's every bit as much a nigger as you or me."

"Sounds like you're better off without her."

"She's singing tonight. Amateur Night at the Apollo. She's been waiting four years for this chance. She told me to spread the word. She needs supporters in the crowd."

"I'll be there. You going?"

"Fuck no. I'm gonna go down to Greenwich Village. Get me a real white girl!"

"Better enjoy this life while we can, huh? We might damn well be drafted soon."

"What the fuck you talkin' about?"

"Pearl Harbor."

"Who she?"

* * *

The Apollo was packed that night. Naturally, Viper Morton was given a choice seat, fifth row center. But no one dared approach him. No one even dared wave hello. One year after West Indian Charlie got his throat slit and Big Al hung himself in his cell, Viper had fulfilled his Machiavellian destiny: feared by all, loved by none. All around him, he heard talk of war. The lights dimmed. Amateur night began. One hopeful singer, one deluded musician, one desperate band after another. Viper pitied them in the same way he pitied his younger self, an ignorant hick just arrived from Meachum, Alabama. He didn't have what it took to be a trumpet player. Pork Chop let him know that real fast, so he'd quit. These amateurs, well, all of them were better than he had been. But still, they had no business thinkin' they could make it. Then came the last contestant of the evening. Viper was so nervous for her, he could hardly breathe.

"Ladies and gentlemen," the emcee announced, "please welcome Yolanda DeVray!"

Yo-Yo looked incandescent in her purple party dress. She strode up to the microphone with an uncanny ease and comfort, totally natural. Like she belonged up there. Like she was born to do this. Then Yo-Yo opened her mouth to sing.

If it was the voice of an angel, then it was one fierce angel, an angel who sweeps down on you with a fiery sword. Yo-Yo slayed the audience with her unique sound, a voice that was both ethereal and earthy, sweet yet sultry, tender but filled with a steamy sensuality. And through the entire song, Yo-Yo seemed to be looking straight at the Viper. When she hit her final, orgiastic note, the entire audience rose to its feet, applauding madly. Viper stood there, clapping hard, fighting back the tears welling in his eyes. Yo-Yo wasn't looking at him anymore. Her eyes slowly scanned the crowd. She was beaming. Drinking in the adulation. This was her baptism.

Minutes later, the emcee thundered: "The winner of tonight's Apollo Theater Amateur Night competition is—by unanimous decision—Yolanda DeVray!"

Backstage, Yo-Yo was mobbed. But when folks saw the Viper jostling his way through the crowd, they abruptly stepped aside.

"Clyde, I'm so glad you came!" Yolanda glowed. "Did you see I was looking at you the whole time?"

"Yes, I did, Yo-Yo."

"Take me away from here!"

Viper took her to the Savoy Ballroom. They had an intimate corner booth. He ordered pink champagne.

"Happy birthday, Yo-Yo."

"Thanks, killer."

"You need to stop calling me that."

"Why? I see who you are."

"And I see you, Yo-Yo."

"What do you see?"

"A great singer. A star."

"A lot of men gave me their business cards tonight. Do you think I should join a band?"

"Depends which one. You could certainly get a place in the house band at Mr. O's club."

"He didn't even show up tonight."

"Mr. O? That's true. I didn't see Pork Chop there either."

"Tell me, Clyde, would you like to be my manager?"

"I don't know that anybody could manage you, Yo-Yo."

"You could. You might be the only man that can manage me."

"We should discuss this in my apartment."

"Let's go."

Yo-Yo made love the way she sang. She gave all of herself to it. Like her singing, her lovemaking was fierce and tender, and Viper had never experienced anything like it. They fell asleep in each other's arms. He awoke to the sound of her gentle weeping.

"Yo-Yo, what's the matter?"

"It's nothing. I should go."

"Am I your first?"

She paused a long time before answering: "No."

"Was it Peewee?"

"No. I already told you I never even let Peewee kiss me."

"All right."

"I should go."

"I'll drive you back to the penthouse."

It was five in the morning. They got in Viper's black Cadillac and headed downtown. Yo-Yo was silent for most of the ride. Finally, she said:

"This is going to be my last day as a maid. When the day is done, I'm gonna pack my bags and walk out of Mr. O's penthouse. I might need a place to stay for a couple of nights before I can find an apartment of my own."

"You can stay with me, Yo-Yo. But people might talk."

"I don't care. Besides, they won't say much. Everybody in Harlem is afraid of you."

"But you're not?"

"Hell no, Clyde. *You* should be afraid of *me*."

"Is that so?"

"Uh-huh."

"Well, I don't scare so easy."

Viper pulled up to the door of Mr. O's building. Yo-Yo kissed him softly on the lips.

"Bye, killer."

*   *   *

A few hours later, sometime mid-morning, Viper was sitting in his basement office, daydreaming about Yo-Yo, when the phone rang. He expected to hear her voice.

"Hello?"

"Hello, Clyde . . . ?"

"Yes?"

"This is Matilda, Mr. O's head maid."

"Matilda? What's the matter?"

"You need to come to the penthouse right away."

"Can you tell me what this is about?"

"No. Just come, please. Right now."

The doorman at Mr. O's building greeted Viper grimly. "Good morning, Mr. Morton."

The elevator operator uttered his usual line in a solemn monotone: "Good morning, sir. I'll take you straight to the top."

When Matilda opened the penthouse door, Viper could see she had been crying.

"Please follow me, Clyde."

There was an eerie quiet in Mr. O's apartment. Matilda led Viper down the marble corridor. They passed through the room with the large wooden table—but none of the joint-rolling maids were there. Matilda then led him into the small, book-lined den, where she opened one of the three doors, a door he had never passed through. The first thing Viper saw in the huge room was a king-size bed with a canopy. The next thing that caught his eye was the body lying dead on the floor.

Mr. O lay on his back, arms spread, eyes wide open, staring lifelessly at the ceiling. His silk bathrobe was open, revealing the bony, pallid nakedness it had luxuriously concealed. There were four gaping gashes in his chest, one at the base of his throat, still oozing blood, staining and soaking into the Persian floor rugs.

"Ucch. Ucch. Ucch."

Viper heard Yolanda before he saw her. The sound was like someone choking. Yolanda was curled up, her body wedged into the far corner, poised in a crouch. She held a letter opener, sharp as a dagger, in her fist. The blade was dripping blood. There was blood on Yo-Yo's hands. Blood on her maid's uniform. Blood streaked in her hair. Her eyes were wide and crazy. Animal. She was like a feral cat. Making these choking sounds.

"Ucch. Ucch. Ucch."

Viper slowly walked across the room, past the over-turned chair and small antique desk, the papers and pens, letters and envelopes, business cards, datebooks, and sundry documents strewn across the rugs. He was close to her now. Yo-Yo looked up at him, wild-eyed. He was not quite sure if she recognized him.

"Yo-Yo, drop the letter opener."

She dropped it. He leaned over, very tenderly took hold of her, lifted her to her feet. He could feel her body shaking all over. This must have been what people meant when they spoke of a state of shock.

"Come with me," Viper whispered. "Slowly. Don't look at him, Yo-Yo."

He walked her carefully across the room, holding her shivering body tucked into his, shielding her face with his hand so that she would not have to see one more time what she had done.

Matilda waited for them in the bedroom doorway. "Come, my angel," she said.

They entered the den. "Matilda, get her out of those clothes," Viper said. "Get her in a hot bath, then put her to bed."

"We're on it, Clyde."

Back out in the marble corridor, one of the other uniformed maids appeared from out of nowhere, took hold of Yo-Yo, and whisked her away.

"Please come with me, Clyde," Matilda said, leading him into the kitchen. The magnitude of all this was just beginning to sicken him.

"Thank you, Clyde," Matilda said. "You've been absolutely heroic, but I still need your help."

"What the hell happened here, Matilda?"

"Yolanda had been Mr. O's daytime girlfriend for two years."

Viper felt as if his head had just burst into flames. His entire head was a ball of fire.

"What?"

"She was well compensated for it."

"You were pimping out your own niece?"

"I resent that word, and I will not be judged by the likes of you, Viper Clyde!"

Viper calmed himself. The head of flames cooled.

"But still you want my help."

"Help Yolanda, Clyde!"

"You still haven't told me what happened."

"I don't know! All I can guess is that she told Mr. O she was quitting today, and he put his hand on her one too many times, I don't know. But she stabbed him to death and wouldn't let anyone get near her, lest she stabbed them, too! Until you came along."

"Mr. O would certainly have had appointments scheduled this afternoon. His datebook was open on the floor. People are going to be wondering where he is."

"You've got to help Yolanda, Clyde. We've got to get rid of this body. Or else they'll send our little Yo-Yo to the electric chair!"

"Calm down!"

"Please help us, Clyde!"

Viper looked around the vast, white-tiled kitchen. He saw the biggest home refrigerator he'd ever seen. The latest electric Frigidaire. He saw a big sharp meat cleaver hanging from a hook on the wall.

"Please, Clyde! I'm beggin' you!"

"Shut the fuck up, Matilda! I've got a plan."

*   *   *

Viper told Matilda exactly what they were going to do. It would be up to her to explain every detail to Mr. O's staff, as well as to the doorman and the elevator operator. He left the building and drove back up to Harlem, called an emergency meeting with Pork Chop and Peewee on the rooftop of their dead boss's nightclub.

"I always liked Mr. O," Pork Chop said, a catch in his voice. "He always treated me fairly, with respect."

"Me too," Peewee said. "And now that crazy bitch has gone and killed him."

"He was trying to rape her," Viper said.

"Oh yeah?" Peewee snarled. "And how much was she gettin' paid to get raped?"

"Whatever you wanna say about it," Pork Chop said, "we gotta get rid of the body."

"Why? Why we gotta save Yolanda? Let her ass fry for this!"

"Don't you get it, Peewee?" Viper said. "If the cops find Mr. O dead in his penthouse, surrounded by nothin' but black folks, they'll investigate all of us."

"He has to disappear," Pork Chop said. "That way the cops will wonder what happened. And they'll probably think it had something to do with Mr. O's dealings downtown, with the I-talian mob."

"At least they won't come straight after us," Viper said.

"I still say y'all just want to protect Yolanda," Peewee said.

"Clyde's got a good plan," Pork Chop said. "We gotta get movin'. Are you with us, Peewee? Or do you want us to throw your tiny ass off this roof right now?"

No one spoke. The three friends heard the flow of traffic six floors below. Pigeons warbled. Seagulls screeched. Peewee seemed to wonder if Pork Chop was serious. Viper could see that Pork Chop was.

Finally, Peewee said: "Guess I'm with you."

A little while later, the three of them pulled up to Mr. O's building in a gray pickup truck. They were disguised, if you will, in gray coveralls and work caps emblazoned with the cursive script logo for "One-Eyed Willie's Junkyard." They walked into the lobby, wheeling a wide, six-foot-tall, empty wooden crate. The doorman acted like he'd never seen any one of them before.

"What can I do for you boys?"

"Mr. Orlinsky's got a busted Frigidaire," Pork Chop said. "We come to take it off his hands."

"You watch how you move that thing, boys," the elevator operator said, perhaps overacting just a bit. "Don't scratch the paneling."

"Oh, am I glad to see you boys!" Matilda said as she swung open the penthouse door. "Come on in."

They parked the crate in the kitchen, and Matilda led them to the bedroom. Viper thought Pork Chop might shed a tear when he saw Mr. O's body, but he was all business. He'd done this sort of thing before.

"Put your work gloves on," he instructed Viper and Peewee, "and help me carry him into the bathroom."

Matilda had already placed the meat cleaver and other tools beside the empty bathtub in which they dumped Mr. O. Viper left the bathroom and let Pork Chop do his work: the hacking and carving, the gutting and the bleeding. Most folks didn't know how Oscar Bradley had gotten his nickname. He'd grown up on a hog farm in Arkansas. Pork Chop knew his way around a slaughter.

While Pork Chop did his job, Viper directed Peewee, Matilda and the maids in the cleanup operation. They cut up the bloody rugs and all the splattered pieces of paper into thousands of little strips and dumped the fragments in burlap sacks, along with Mr. O's silk bathrobe and Yolanda's maid uniform. They rearranged other Persian rugs, clean ones. They uprighted the chair and antique desk. They scrubbed all the bloodstains from the furniture. They scoured and polished the deadly letter opener.

"Anything we've forgotten?" Matilda asked.

"I don't think so," Viper said. Peewee had left the bedroom to go check in on Pork Chop. Viper took the occasion to ask Matilda, "How is Yolanda?"

"Fast asleep. I gave her a pill. We've got her booked on a train to New Orleans at eight tomorrow morning."

"All right. Give her my best."

"You're saving her life, Clyde. God bless you."

The maids had emptied and unplugged the Frigidaire. Viper, Pork Chop, and Peewee replenished it with Mr. O's body parts, then loaded it into the crate and wheeled it out of the lobby.

"So long, boys!" the doorman said, his voice overcome by a wave of relief.

They drove to One-Eyed Willie's Junkyard, in the most desolate corner of Harlem.

"Welcome," the old junkman said, squinting with his good eye, the other one rolling about like a marble in a milky sack.

Behind a barbed-wire fence was a small village of rusted cars, bedframes, and every manner of scrap metal. They wheeled the crate into the middle of the wasteland. They pulled the Frigidaire out of the crate.

"Thanks, Willie," Viper said.

"We'll wait till nightfall," Willie said. "That's when the dogs come out."

Viper, Pork Chop, and Peewee made a trash-can fire. They burned Mr. O's bathrobe, Yolanda's uniform, and the cut-up strips of bloody bedroom rugs and papers. As night fell, they watched from the other side of the fence as One-Eyed Willie opened the Frigidaire, and the junkyard dogs came swarming and snarling, devouring the flesh and gnawing on the bones Willie tossed to them.

"All right, fellas," Pork Chop said. "Go home and try to sleep."

*   *   *

Viper didn't sleep at all. He lay in bed, thinking about Yolanda. And Mr. O. His hands on her. He should have guessed it before, but he hadn't wanted to see what was plain in front of him. But what could have made Yolanda go at Mr. O with the letter opener like that? And now she was fleeing back to New Orleans. After her triumph at the Apollo. After their passionate night together. So much promise. Gone. Viper needed to see her one last time. Matilda said Yolanda's train was leaving at eight. He decided to go to the station. At seven o'clock, he was dressed and heading out the door.

"Hello, Viper." Detective Red Carney was waiting outside his building, with two goons in uniform. "Where's Mr. O?"

"At this hour? Home in bed, I guess."

"As a matter of fact, he's been missing since yesterday."

"You don't say."

"Viper, you're under arrest. For suspicion of the murder of Abraham Orlinsky."

An hour later, as Yo-Yo's train was leaving the station, Viper was chained to a metal chair in Carney's small, nondescript office. The young cop paced back and forth, his face living up to his nickname, scarlet with panic and rage.

"Red," Viper said, "you're barking up the wrong tree."

"Don't mess with me, nigger!" Red screamed, spraying saliva. "I don't know exactly what happened, but I do know that you and Peewee and Pork Chop are in deep shit. I've got the two of them under arrest as well."

"What have you got on us?"

Viper's calm tone seemed to calm Red Carney. The cop stopped pacing. He paused, then spoke evenly, as if figuring out a plan that was just becoming clear in his fevered brain.

"Frankly, nothing," Carney said. "Except the fact that you're three niggers suspected of having been criminal accomplices of Mr. O's, so no matter who killed him, we can blame it on you chumps. Open and shut case. That said, there are plenty of people who might be glad to see Mr. O suddenly gone and many others who might very well have made him disappear. So there is one way out for you and Peewee and Pork Chop, only one way for you three black chumps to avoid taking the fall for some mafioso down in Little Italy."

"And what's that?"

"To serve your country."

"Enlist?"

"Or go to trial. For murder. All three of you."

And that is how Pork Chop Bradley wound up serving as a janitor in an Army barracks in Texas for the duration of the Second World War. As for Viper and Peewee, they both wound up in the Navy, serving as kitchen workers and haulers on different battleships in the Pacific.

"I'm thinking of joining up myself, Viper," Red Carney continued. "If Mr. O really has been rubbed out, there's gonna be a shitstorm in New York. I'd just as soon get away from it."

*　　*　　*

Looking back on his life, from the vantage point of Nica's Cathouse couch, on the night of his third murder, in November 1961, Viper's first killing still lingered in his mind. He didn't regret slashing West Indian Charlie's throat. It had been a sound business decision. But he'd never stopped wondering if, just before he'd silenced him, Charlie had hissed a voodoo curse on his ass.

One of the curiosities of the Viper's gangster reputation was that folks believed he'd killed more people than he actually had. To this day, a lot of folks thought Viper Morton had executed Abraham Orlinsky. Twenty years after Mr. O's death, remembering how he had saved Yolanda, Viper picked up the notepad and scribbled his second wish.

I wish she had loved me.

6

HARLEM WAS ALWAYS ON HIS mind. He thought about the place all day, dreamt about it every night. Through four years of war in the Pacific, perversely called "the Pacific Theater," as if it was supposed to be entertaining, Viper Morton—in his mind, whether in his waking hours or his restless sleep—never left Harlem.

Viper and his fellow black sailors on the battleship were known, officially, as Steward's Mates. It was a fancy new term for what had traditionally been called "mess hall attendants." This was all that most "colored" sailors were considered good for. Viper spent four years slingin' hash, taking orders, washing dishes and pots and pans, and taking orders, mopping kitchen floors, donning a white tunic and waiting on the tables in the officers' dining hall, and taking orders—from white men who never called him anything but "boy."

In his mind, he was cruising down Lenox Avenue in his big black Cadillac, one hand relaxed on the steering wheel, the other resting on the rolled-down window of the driver's side door, sunlight glinting off the diamond-studded, horseshoe-shaped cufflinks he'd picked out at Braunstein's department store. His memories of the ribs and cornbread at the Red Rooster were more real to him than the Navy slop he ate for four years. As he scrubbed the ship's toilets, he felt a strange sense of disbelief. In his mind, he was in the basement of Gentleman Jack's barbershop, distributing twelve-joint packets of gage to his small army of dealers, counting stacks of money.

In four years, Viper never saw combat. But he heard it, as he and the other black steward's mates were made to haul heavy equipment and ammunition through the bowels of the ship while outside cannons blasted and warplanes screeched in the sky or whistled in downward spirals before splashing in thunderous explosions in the ocean.

Somehow, it wasn't real to the Viper. What seemed more vivid, almost tangible, were his visions of Yolanda: Yo-Yo beaming, arms spread wide, soaking in the applause on the stage of the Apollo Theater; radiant as she clinked champagne glasses with him at the Savoy Ballroom; fierce and tender as their naked bodies writhed in his bed. And more horrific than the sounds of war outside the suffocating walls of the battleship: the sight of Yolanda, bloody dagger-like weapon in her hand, blood on her maid's uniform, blood in her hair, crouching, wild-eyed and feral, in Mr. O's bedroom.

Where was she now? New Orleans?

What was she doing? Was she singing?

Was she thinking of him? Would he ever see her again, his beautiful, dangerous Yo-Yo?

Four years trapped in a giant, floating sardine can. He didn't even allow himself to think that someday this war would end. Then, suddenly, it did.

KABOOM! Payback in Hiroshima. When Viper first heard about the atomic bomb the new president, Harry Truman, had dropped, he thought: "Damn, that's a gangster move." Then, a couple of days later, Truman doubled down with a bomb dropped on Nagasaki. Even as revenge for Pearl Harbor, it seemed extreme. Hardcore gangster. But he couldn't argue with results. Three months after the twin mushroom clouds unfurled over Japan, Clyde "the Viper" Morton was on his way back to Harlem.

*   *   *

I am speaking now of late November 1945. Viper directed his taxi driver to drop him off right in front of his brownstone on Lenox Avenue. Dressed in his ridiculous sailor's suit, duffel bag slung over his shoulder, Viper bounded up the stairs to his apartment, imagining nothing had changed in four years. He tried to stick his key in the lock. It didn't fit. Damn it. He rang the doorbell. No answer. Banged on the door. Silence. He went back down the stairs. Stood still on the sidewalk. That's when it hit him.

This wasn't the Viper's Harlem anymore. People bustled down the street, traffic flowed along the avenue, but something had changed. Everything felt quieter, more subdued. He didn't recognize anybody on the streets. And nobody seemed to remember him. He felt almost invisible. Once folks in Harlem had looked upon the Viper with love, then with fear. Now, they didn't even see him. He had become a ghost.

He wandered around the neighborhood. The street-corner exhorters were still speechifying on their stepladders and barrels, preachers warning about Judgment Day, young communists envisioning a workers' utopia, black separatists urging a return to the paradise of Africa. But even they seemed to lack the intensity they had back in the day. Viper meandered aimlessly until he came upon a sight that stopped him cold. He stood in front of a block that looked like a photo of war-torn Europe: the charred remains of bombed-out buildings. In the center of the street loomed the shattered and burned bulbs of the old neon sign of the department store: BRAUNSTEIN'S. Viper peered through the gaping holes where picture windows once sparkled. He could see, through the debris, the smashed remnants of the jewelry counter.

Viper trudged up Seventh Avenue toward Gentleman Jack's. The bell above the door tinkled as he entered. The barbershop was as quiet as a funeral parlor. No customers at all. A couple of barbers sat in their chairs, reading newspapers. Two others were off in the corner, playing checkers. Gentleman Jack himself was asleep in his throne-like barber's chair. He looked like he'd aged more than four years. Viper whispered in his ear.

"Psst, Jack . . ."

The old barber awoke with a start. "Viper Clyde, is that you?"

"How are you, Jack?"

"Take off that sailor cap. Lemme see your head . . . Oh yeah, you could use a good conk. Have a seat, son."

Viper couldn't help wincing as the sizzling lye hit his scalp.

"What's goin' on, Jack? Everything seems . . . kind of sad."

"Yeah, Viper, it's been like that since the riots two years ago. White cop shot a black soldier. All hell broke loose.

Fires. Looting. Six people dead. It was a damn nightmare. Some blocks still haven't been cleaned up."

"Yeah, I just walked by Braunstein's."

"Tsk, tsk, tsk." Gentleman Jack sucked his teeth and shook his head grimly. "That store was a big target. Arthur Jr. lost everything that night. Couple of weeks later, he shot himself in the head."

"Damn."

"Yeah, Viper, like you said, sad. Harlem has never recovered. Ain't many popular nightclubs left. The jazz scene has moved down to 52nd Street."

"What? Midtown?"

"White folks are too scared to come up to Harlem now. All the hot clubs are on one block along 52nd Street: the Three Deuces, the Carousel, the Onyx. But the music has changed, Viper."

"What do you mean, 'changed'?"

"There's a new style called bebop, or rebop, or zebop. Crazy people's music. It's played really fast, but it don't swing. You can't dance to it. You're supposed to sit and listen to it like it's Beethoven or something, but it sounds like a bunch of random notes. It's just noise."

"You jivin' me?"

"Hell no, Viper. This is what all the young fellas wanna play. You ever hear of Charlie Parker?"

"Nope."

"Sax player outta Kansas City. Nicknamed Bird. Ever hear of a trumpet player called Dizzy Gillespie?"

"Nope."

"How about Thelonious Monk?"

"What? Is that somebody's name?"

"Piano player. These are the young bucks of bebop. Or whatever it's called. And they're all a bunch of junkies."

"They are?"

"Smack is everywhere, Viper. It's a damn shame."

"And reefer?"

"Sure, it's around. But we don't got anything goin' like we had back in the day. We ain't dealin' outta the shop anymore. Not since you all disappeared."

"What do you mean 'disappeared'?"

"What do I mean? Pearl Harbor happens one day, and two days later, Mr. O vanishes into thin air. And the day after that, you, Pork Chop, and Peewee all vanish. Red Carney came around, seized all the gage we had here. Then he vanished, too. Joined the army, I heard."

"And who owns your shop now?"

"Mr. O's law firm took over all his properties. They shut down the nightclub, though. It's been boarded up for four years."

"Any news of Peewee?"

"None. Pork Chop is back in town, though. I heard he's working at a recording studio downtown."

"Really? As a session man?"

"No, as a janitor."

"Right." Viper paused, took a deep breath. "Listen, Jack, I'd like to ask you about a job—for me."

"Oh, Viper, I ain't got no need for a business manager. And I told you, we ain't dealin' gage no more."

"No, Jack, I'd like you to hire me as a barber."

"Really? You, Viper?"

"I need a job, Jack. An honest job."

"Well, all right. I'll give you Big Al's old station."

Viper turned his head and saw the empty barber's chair and the clean counter in front of it. Big Al's station—where, five years earlier, he had slit West Indian Charlie's throat.

"You can start tomorrow," Gentleman Jack said.

*   *   *

Viper checked into the same cheap boardinghouse where he'd stayed when he first arrived in Harlem back in '36, a country boy from Meachum, Alabama. He emptied his duffel bag, took off his sailor's suit for the last time, and changed into civilian clothes.

The next day, after the end of his first day's work as a barber, he went down to WOR Studios to look for Pork Chop. He spotted his oldest friend in New York walking down a long corridor, carrying a mop and a bucket. Pork Chop didn't notice Viper. He was still round and bearish, still wore his fedora with the front brim snapped up. He stopped in front of a closet, stored the mop and bucket, and only then did he see Viper, standing a few feet in front of him. They did not embrace. They did not shake hands.

"How are you, Clyde?"

"I'm all right, Pork Chop. How was your war?"

"I spent it cleanin' toilets at a base in Texas. Heard you and Peewee were in the Pacific."

"Yeah, any word from the l'il man?"

"Nothin' yet."

"What about Yolanda?"

"Far as I know, she went back to New Orleans and entered a convent."

"What? Yo-Yo's gonna be a nun?"

"Guilt will do that to you. I still think of Mr. O. The sound of them dogs."

"You're too sentimental, Pork Chop." Viper didn't know why, really, but he felt he had to feign a hard-boiled attitude.

"You don't think about it?" Pork Chop said. "What we did to protect Yolanda?"

"Not much," Viper brazenly lied. "Let's go get a drink."

"Naw, man, I was about to sit in on a session. You gotta hear the new music, Clyde. Come with me."

Pork Chop led Viper into a recording studio and introduced him to a fat, sweaty white guy. "Clyde Morton, this is the producer, Teddy Reig."

"Pleased to meet ya," Reig said.

On the other side of the wide window of the control booth, Viper saw the musicians fiddling with their instruments.

"All right, fellas," Reig said into a microphone, "whenever you're ready."

The band launched into a song Viper didn't recognize. Viper was instantly astonished. Awestruck. He'd never heard anything like this style of playing. The dexterity. The velocity. The modernity. He perceived it all very clearly, right away, in that recording studio. It was 1945. A new age had been born. And this would be its music.

"The big guy on the sax," Pork Chop whispered, "that's Charlie Parker."

"Folks call him Bird, right?" Viper asked.

"Exactly. The guy with the beret is Dizzy Gillespie. Normally he's on trumpet, but he's playing piano today 'cause Bud Powell, the pianist, didn't show up."

"Who's the skinny kid with the trumpet?"

"Miles Davis. Rich Negro from East Saint Louis. His daddy's a dentist. The fella on bass is Curley Russell and the drummer is Max Roach."

"I heard all of the beboppers are into heroin."

"Well, I don't know about *that*. Bird's a serious junkie. Hardcore. He also happens to be a genius. So a lot of the young cats copy him. They think that to play like Bird, you gotta shoot up like Bird. It's gettin' bad, Viper. But the music. Wow."

Viper left the studio feeling dazed, dazzled. He barely slept that night.

The next afternoon, he sat in Big Al's old barber's chair, still waiting for his first customer of the day, feeling as if life had just passed him by. Harlem had changed. Jazz itself had changed. Viper Morton was only twenty-eight years old. But he suddenly felt like he was obsolete. And then . . .

The bell above the barbershop door tinkled, and a familiar high-pitched voice cried: "Wake up, you lazy motherfuckers!"

In walked Peewee. The little man was dressed in a zoot suit: oversized jacket, baggy pants, a long watch chain swinging from his pants pocket as he strutted across the barbershop floor, a floppy, wide-brimmed hat on his head.

"Viper Clyde Morton," Peewee squealed, "who told you you was a barber? I talked to three fellas whose heads you fucked up yesterday. They ashamed to leave the house, you messed up they conks so bad."

"Nice to see you too, Peewee. How long you been back?"

"Damn near a month already, but I ain't been hangin' out with you niggas up in Harlem. All the action is down on 52nd Street. And I'm shackin' up with a white chick down in Greenwich Village."

"You're lookin' sharp, my man."

"Wish I could say the same for you, Viper. Get outta that barber's tunic. You're comin' with me. You don't mind if I take this chump off your hands, do ya, Gentleman Jack?"

"You'll be doin' me a favor," Jack said. "Sorry, Viper, but as a barber, you're no Big Al."

"Get a move on, nigga," Peewee said. "We got people waitin' for us."

"What people? Where?"

"We goin' back into the reefer business."

* * *

As they walked through the streets of Harlem, Viper had no idea where Peewee was taking him. He was just glad to see him again.

"Any news from Yolanda?" Peewee asked.

"Pork Chop says she joined a convent," Viper said.

"Yeah, he told me that same shit. You believe him?"

"Pork Chop also said he hadn't heard from *you*."

"He hadn't till this morning. And here he is now."

They arrived at Mr. O's nightclub. The facade was hidden behind a metal grate. Standing in front of the club were three men: Pork Chop Bradley, Detective Red Carney, and another white man: young, thin, and pale, wearing a somber suit and thick eyeglasses.

"Well, hello, Viper Clyde."

"Hello, Detective Carney. How was your war?"

"Not so bad. Killed a lot of Germans. Let me introduce you to Dan Miller of the law firm Schneider, Miller, and Bloom."

"Mr. O's firm," Viper said.

He and the lawyer shook hands.

"Yes, my father, Myron Miller was a close adviser to Abraham Orlinsky. I'm back from the war and have just joined the firm. My father has handed over much of the Orlinsky dossier to me."

"Turns out Mr. O left a will, Clyde," Pork Chop said.

"Yeah," Carney said, "but you and Pork Chop aren't in it."

Dan Miller said, "The nightclub has been bequeathed to Mr. Peter Woodrow Robinson."

The gaunt, young lawyer handed Peewee the keys to the club.

"Thanks, Miller," Peewee said. "Just so y'all know, once we reopen the club, I'm changing the name from Mr. O's to Peewee's."

The proud new proprietor unlocked the metal grate and rolled it up.

"Where can we discuss business?" Dan Miller asked.

"Follow me upstairs, gents," Peewee said.

Viper felt a rush when he stepped out onto the rooftop. The vast Harlem sky. The sound of warbling pigeons, the traffic below. This was where he had met his destiny, where Pork Chop Bradley had introduced him to Mary Warner, nearly ten years earlier.

"So, gentlemen," Dan Miller said, "all signs indicate that the market for marijuana is going to continue to expand. Mr. O's Harlem monopoly on Mexican locoweed has been broken up among a number of dealers. But we're not concerned with Mexico. Under our new business plan, the supply will be originating in California. Our firm is connected with a large marijuana farm near San Francisco."

"It's concealed amid a bunch of vineyards in the Sonoma Valley wine country," Red Carney said.

"And it's some good shit, too," Peewee said. He pulled out a joint, lit it up, took a drag, then held the stick out to the lawyer. "Miller?"

"No, thanks. I don't smoke."

"I'll take a hit," Red Carney said. "I don't go on duty for another two hours." The ruddy cop sucked hungrily on the joint.

"Once the new nightclub opens," Dan Miller said, "that will be our base of operations. Gage will be delivered by truck, boxloads of joints, marked as ordinary restaurant supplies. We'd like you to return as leader of the house band, Mr. Bradley."

"My pleasure," Pork Chop said. "May I have a hit off that joint, Detective?"

"I didn't forget you, Pork Chop," Carney said, coughing and passing the stick.

"And we'd like you to take the title of business manager of the club, Mr. Morton," Miller said.

"That means I'd be your boss, Viper," Peewee said.

"Actually," Miller said, "your salary would be paid by the firm of Schneider, Miller, and Bloom. You'd run a network of dealers, just as you did so efficiently out of the barbershop before the war. And we're doubling the price. We'll be selling joints at a dollar apiece, ten dollars for a dozen."

"Whoa," Pork Chop said. "That's some powerful shit. Take a hit before you say yes, Viper."

"Always good to know the product," Viper said, raising the joint to his lips. *Ssssss . . .*

"And I'll provide cover with the law," Carney said, "just like I did back in the day."

Viper exhaled, paused for a moment as he waited for the high to kick in. "That's an excellent product," he said. "But I heard all the young musicians are into heroin."

"We don't want any part of that business," Dan Miller said. "We'll be dealing gage exclusively."

"That's good," Viper said. "Because I refuse to sell junk."

"Mr. O told my father how you feel about heroin," Miller said. "We will not be dealing it. You have my word."

"All right, then."

"And, oh," the young lawyer added, "our firm has dealings with the owner of your old building on Lenox Avenue. We can get you your old apartment back, Mr. Morton."

"Thanks, Miller," Viper said, feeling genuinely touched. "I appreciate that."

The five men shook hands all around.

"Peewee's is gonna be the hippest club in Harlem," Peewee said. "Right now, there's only one club up here that's worth going to: Minton's Playhouse. It's where all the beboppers jam after hours. I'll take you there tonight, Viper."

*   *   *

Peewee and Viper walked into Minton's Playhouse, in the basement of the Cecil Hotel on 118th Street, at two in the morning. The club was crowded, hot, and rollicking. Viper heard sounds coming from a piano unlike any he'd heard before: jagged, complex, exuberant, utterly modern.

"That's Thelonious Monk on the piano," Peewee said.

"Damn," Viper said. "These beboppers can play. His piano sounds like Bird's saxophone. Is he a junkie too?"

"Never heard that he was," Peewee said. "Monk's a dedicated viper, though. And forget drugs. Monk was just born a crazy motherfucker."

A small table opened up. Viper and Peewee sat down and ordered drinks. Viper noticed a slick-looking cat waving at them as he pushed his way through the crowd toward their table. He was strikingly handsome in a ginger-toned, delicate way. And he had that special aura about him. You could tell he was a star.

"That's Pretty Paul Baxter," Peewee told Viper. "Great vocalist. The ladies love him. They call him the sepia Sinatra. But he's a bebopper all the way. And heavy into junk."

"Peewee!" Pretty Paul said, grasping the little man's hand and pumping it with the stiff enthusiasm of a politician on the stump. "So glad to see you, man! I'm on next, with my new band."

"Solid," Peewee said. "Let me introduce you to Clyde Morton."

"Clyde Morton?" Pretty Paul said. "Viper Morton? *The* Viper?"

"You've heard of me?" Viper said.

"You're a legend!" Pretty Paul grasped Viper's hand, and now the enthusiasm of the vigorous pumping was genuine. "Such an honor to meet you, sir!"

"We're opening up a new club," Peewee said. "Gonna be called Peewee's."

"Congrats, man! We should celebrate. How 'bout we all go to Buttercup's place?"

"That poof?" Viper said.

Viper remembered Buttercup Jones from before the war. Cotton Club dancer, turned tricks in the men's toilet with white customers whose wives sat obliviously in the dance hall, listening to the orchestra.

"Buttercup runs the best whorehouse in Harlem. How long you been back, Viper?"

"Three days."

"So you must be horny as a motherfucker."

"Horny for a woman, yeah."

"What the fuck you think I'm talkin' about?" Paul said indignantly.

"Uh-oh," Peewee said. "Looks like Viper took Pretty Paul for a fairy."

"Buttercup's hos are the finest in Harlem," Paul said. "And they are *all* women. Ask around, Viper: everybody knows Pretty Paul is *only* into pussy."

"Sorry, Paul," Viper said.

"Hell, I'm even married. Keep my wife in the house, cookin' and cleanin', so I can be free to run around, gettin' all the pussy I can grab."

"And now," the emcee announced, "ladies and gentlemen . . ."

"See you after the gig, Viper," Paul said. "You comin' with us, Peewee?"

The emcee continued: ". . . especially you ladies . . . the act you've been waiting for . . ."

"Naw, man," Peewee said. "I got my blond-haired, blue-eyed Sally waitin' for me down in the Village."

"Pretty Paul Baxter!"

Paul leapt from the table, strode through the crowd, and bounded onto the stage. He was a highly polished performer. Smooooooth. Rich timbre baritone. Could probably croon with the best of them, but he was bopping tonight. Finger-snapping rhythm-a-ning with riffs, impeccable scatting. The crowd ate it up.

It was nearly five in the morning when Pretty Paul and Viper left Minton's and headed toward the brownstone on 112th Street, where Buttercup Jones ran his whorehouse.

"You know," Paul said, "I've dealt a fair amount of weed the past year or so. If you really are going back into the business, I'd love to work for you."

"Well, Paul, if you're as good a dealer as you are a singer, consider yourself hired."

"Thanks, Viper! You're even cooler than everybody said you were."

Pretty Paul pressed the buzzer, and Buttercup Jones himself opened the front door. "Well, Viper Clyde, you are a sight for sore eyes!"

"Hello, Buttercup."

"And welcome, Pretty Paul! You're becoming quite the regular, aren't you?"

Buttercup must have been pushing fifty, but he still had the lean, lithe body of a dancer. He was even more effeminate than Viper had remembered. Buttercup wore a sort of Oriental house gown, an elaborate pompadour hairdo, and heavy lipstick and mascara. He led them into what he called the "salon." It was a dimly lit room, dotted with ravishing women in satin slips and silk robes.

"Gather 'round, ladies," Pretty Paul announced as they entered the room. "This here is Clyde 'the Viper' Morton. He's a Harlem legend. Just back from the Pacific Theater. You ladies gotta show him a proper homecomin'."

Pretty Paul hadn't lied. These had to be the finest hos in Harlem. Buttercup walked up to Viper with a glass of champagne and a joint.

"Here, Viper," the pimp said, "you'll recognize this Mexican locoweed. And by the way, for you, everything tonight is on the house."

"Thanks, Buttercup."

Viper watched as Buttercup sauntered over to Paul and handed him a little, square, wax-paper packet.

"Hey, Buttercup, you know I ain't got . . ."

"No worries, Paul, I'll put it on your tab."

"Solid. Thanks, baby."

"Come with me, Clyde," a shapely hooker who called herself Jezebel purred in the Viper's ear. "Let me show you how much I love Navy men." She led him to a bedroom down the hall. Within seconds they were naked and humping on top of the bed. Viper was high and making love to a beautiful woman. Finally, it felt good to be back in Harlem.

* * *

"Hey, Viper, wake up."

Viper slowly opened his eyes. Jezebel lay on the bed, naked beside him, fast asleep, slightly snoring. "Huh, what?" he muttered.

"Viper, wake up," someone said again.

Viper turned around and saw Pretty Paul, fully clothed, standing above the bed. Sunlight streamed through the window of the whorehouse bedroom. "Let's go to my place. I'll have my wife make us breakfast."

Out on the streets of Harlem, early risers were starting their days. Pretty Paul Baxter and Viper Morton walked up St. Nicholas Avenue, hands in pockets, shoulders hunched against the morning chill, a little high, a little hungover, and definitely hungry.

"You sure your wife won't mind a stranger dropping in, asking to be fed?" Viper said.

"Hell, no," Paul said. "She's used to cookin' breakfast for me after I been out all night. She'll do as she's told. Ain't you ever been married, Viper?"

"Naw, man, never met a woman who would stay at home and cook and clean like yours."

"Oh, you gotta get one, Viper. Just make sure she always knows who's the boss."

As soon as they entered the apartment, Paul shouted down the hallway: "Woman! Wake up. We got company. Get out here and cook us some breakfast."

Viper heard a muffled, faraway voice respond, the words unintelligible. "Listen, Paul," Viper said, "maybe I should just go back to the boarding house."

"No, come on in." Paul led Viper to the kitchen. "Here, have a seat. You want some coffee?"

"Listen, Paul, I . . ."

Paul leaned out the kitchen door, yelled down the hallway again. "Woman, get your ass in here!" He turned back to the Viper. "Lemme see what we got in the icebox. How 'bout steak and eggs and some grits? What's takin' that bitch so long?"

"Paul, you'll wake the neighbors," Mrs. Baxter said as she entered the kitchen, still dressed in her plaid bathrobe.

"Yolanda!" Viper gasped.

"Clyde!" Yolanda cried.

Pretty Paul looked puzzled. "You two know each other?"

"Yes," Viper and Yolanda said in unison, stunned.

* * *

It occurred to Viper that it was a good thing he was sitting down. He felt like he might swoon, staggered by the sight of Yolanda, her honey-gold skin, her emerald eyes. She looked distinctly older, less girlish and more womanly. But even more beautiful, sexier than ever, even in her plaid bathrobe.

"You made it back," Yolanda said.

"So did you," Viper said.

"What you waitin' for, Yolanda?" Paul said. "Cook us some damn breakfast."

"Yes, Paul," Yolanda said sweetly. "What would you like?"

"Steak and eggs and grits. But first, fix us a pot of coffee."

"Yes, Paul." Yolanda got to work, and Pretty Paul winked at their guest.

"Like I told you, Viper. You gotta show 'em who's boss."

Pretty Paul prattled on. Viper thought he was mainly talking about his singing career, but he wasn't listening. He felt like he was in some strange dream as he watched Yo-Yo make them breakfast in her plaid bathrobe. She laid two full plates in front of them.

"Here you go, fellas," she said.

"Thanks, Yo-Yo," Viper said.

"Yo-Yo?" Paul said. "Is that what you called her?"

"It's my old nickname," Yolanda said.

"Yo-Yo?" Paul sneered.

"It's a term of endearment, Paul," Viper said.

"Is it now?"

"I have to get dressed," Yolanda said.

"Bring me my kit first," Paul ordered his wife. "Leave it on the coffee table."

Paul and the Viper ate their breakfast in a tense silence. Once they finished, Paul led his guest to the living room. As instructed, Yolanda had laid out his kit on the coffee table: the syringe, the spoon, the rubber tube to wrap around his arm. Paul reached into his jacket and pulled out the little wax-paper packet that Buttercup Jones had handed him at the whorehouse.

"Have a seat, Viper. You wanna shoot up?"

"Naw, man, I don't do that shit."

"Why not? It's the same thing as reefer."

"No, it ain't, Paul. I think you know it ain't."

"Suit yourself."

Viper watched as Pretty Paul prepared his fix, carefully stuck the needle in his vein. He leaned back on the couch, sighed contentedly. He pulled out the needle and didn't say anything for a long time. When he spoke again, his voice had turned sleepy.

"Yeah, Yolanda don't shoot up either," he said. "And she don't smoke reefer. And she don't drink. And she don't go to clubs. She just stays home and looks after me. Ain't that sweet?"

"Yeah, that's real sweet, Paul."

"But in bed, man. Yolanda in bed. Lemme tell you . . ."

Pretty Paul's voice trailed off. Soon he was snoring. Yolanda appeared in the doorway, fully dressed.

"Is he out?" she asked.

"Yeah," Viper said.

"Let's take a walk, Clyde."

*   *   *

Yolanda led the Viper to Riverside Park. The early morning chill had disappeared. The day had turned unseasonably balmy for late November. Yolanda looked chic in a beige cashmere coat. Little black girls were doing Double Dutch in the park, chanting while they skipped rope with exquisite grace, their pigtails bouncing.

"I'm so happy to see you, Clyde," Yolanda said. "I was scared that you were either dead or in jail."

"And I heard you had joined a convent in New Orleans."

They both laughed lightly.

"Yeah, that's a lie my Aunt Matilda put out there. She was just trying to protect me. She figured whoever might want to come after me, be it cops or mobsters, saying I had joined a convent would give me cover. No one would ever believe that a future nun would have had anything to do with what happened to Mr. O."

"And what *did* happen, Yolanda?"

"Mr. O was having his way with me. For two years. I hated it, Clyde. Every minute of it. But Mr. O was obsessed with me. And that last day, when I told him I was quitting for good, he started screaming and sobbing. Then I told him that I had spent the night with you. That's when he really went crazy. He was strangling me. Said if he couldn't have me, nobody would. Least of all, a thug like you. I thought he was gonna choke me to death, Clyde. That's when I grabbed hold of the, the whatchamacallit."

"The letter opener."

"Yeah. I was fighting for my life, Clyde. But the law would never have believed that. They'd have sent me to the electric chair. I know what you and Peewee and Pork Chop did to save me. Matilda told me everything. I don't know how I can ever thank you enough, Clyde."

When Yolanda said those words, Viper thought he would melt. But he couldn't show her that. He wanted to get the lowdown. He played it hard-boiled.

"So, what *did* you do when you got back to New Orleans?"

"I moved back in with my parents. Then, something else bad happened."

"What?"

"I learned I was pregnant."

"Mine?"

"No, Clyde, that would have been wonderful. But I was already pregnant that night we spent together. I just didn't know it yet. And I couldn't bear to have Mr. O's baby. I just couldn't do it. I had a . . . procedure."

"I'm sorry, Yo-Yo."

They stopped walking and sat down on a park bench.

"My parents were so ashamed," Yolanda said, fighting back tears. "They're good people. Simple, honest. They've worked their whole lives at the post office. Devout Catholics. I felt like such a disgrace. Anyway, I eventually took a job as a file clerk at an orphanage run by the Church. So, I didn't become a nun. But I did try to make up for my sins."

"You were more sinned against, Yo-Yo."

"Thank you for saying so."

"And what about your singing?"

"I gave it up."

"But why?"

"It was just a silly kid's ambition."

"No, no! My trumpet playing was a silly kid's ambition. You are gifted, Yo-Yo! Everybody at the Apollo heard it that night! You need to sing."

"No, Clyde, I am devoted to Paul's career. I'm here to support *his* singing."

"Pretty Paul's good," Viper said. "I heard him last night. But damn, Yo-Yo, you're at least as talented as he is. More so."

"I'm here to serve him, Clyde. That's my role."

"How did you two meet?"

"He's from New Orleans. Our parents are friends. I hadn't seen him since I was a little girl. But he was touring with his band last year. Came by the house, charmed my parents. He swept me off my feet, Clyde. But sometimes I think I was just desperate to get out of my parents' house. And to get back to New York. Paul proposed marriage, I said yes, next thing I knew, I was back in Harlem and pregnant again."

"You and Paul have a child?"

"No, Clyde, I had a miscarriage. About three months ago."

"Aw, Yo-Yo, I'm so sorry."

That was when he put his arm around her. He thought she might pull away from him, but she leaned in, snuggled into his shoulder. The scent of her brought back an intoxicating memory of the night they'd made love four years earlier.

"Paul doesn't know about the abortion. My doctor at Harlem Hospital says the procedure might have been botched by the person who did it down in New Orleans. I might not ever be able to carry a pregnancy to term. But Paul doesn't know that. He just desperately wants to have kids. And I just want to make him happy."

"It sounds to me like you're trying to punish yourself. For the sins you think you committed. You want to give up singing. Devote yourself to a less talented singer who treats you like dirt."

Viper felt Yolanda's body stiffen in his embrace. "When did you become Dr. Freud?"

"And Paul's a junkie. What have you got yourself into, Yo-Yo?"

Now she pulled away from him, sat up straight on the bench.

"I don't like your tone."

"Listen, Peewee, Pork Chop, and me, we're gonna reopen Mr. O's nightclub. Gonna call it Peewee's. And we'll be dealing marijuana outta there. We're gonna make a lot of money, Yo-Yo. You say all you want is to make Paul happy. Well, all I want is to make *you* happy. What can I do to make you happy?"

"Is that what you really want, Clyde, to make me happy?"

"Yes."

"Then give Paul work. Singing at the club and dealing gage."

"All right. If that's what you want, I'll do it."

"Thank you, Clyde. And thank you for saving my life."

"Anytime, Yo-Yo. Anytime."

O F ALL THE HUNDRED OR so felines slinking, purring, climbing, prowling, scratching at the furniture,
rolling about the floor and licking themselves, only one at
the Cathouse approached the Viper as he sat on the couch
in the baroness's sprawling living room, contemplating
the third of his three wishes on this night in November 1961. He had gotten quite stoned on the joint he had
treated himself to earlier. This was the product everyone
at the Cathouse was smoking tonight, a superb breed of
marijuana, imported—or smuggled, if you prefer—from
Thailand. He slowly looked around the room. There were
still roughly twenty jazzmen scattered about, talking,
drinking, eating, smoking, fiddling with their instruments, riffin' while relaxin'. Pork Chop Bradley sat in a
far corner, plucking his bass, his eyes closed. He looked
almost like a man at prayer. Thelonious Monk hadn't
moved since they arrived at the Cathouse—Viper, Monk,
and the baroness—in Nica's Bentley. Viper didn't know,
but he could have guessed that Nica had been driving
around Harlem specifically to find him, the reefer man.

She had a houseful of musicians waiting back across the bridge in New Jersey, and she was running low on weed. Now Monk sat as still as a statue in his armchair. He clearly didn't feel like conversing or playing the piano. He just continued to sit there in his silk Chinese beanie, glowering benignly.

The baroness stood before one of the Cathouse's huge picture windows, immersed in quiet conversation with Miles Davis, the Manhattan skyline glittering across the river. Nica was smoking, her trademark cigarette holder clenched between her teeth. Miles was still wearing his pitch-black sunglasses. He pulled on the joint Viper had given him free of charge. Viper had so much respect for Miles. After he'd managed to quit his heroin habit, and once he'd formed his own bands, Miles could not abide the musicians he worked with abusing junk. Not even the great John Coltrane.

"I didn't have no moral thing about Trane and all of them shooting heroin," Miles once said, "because I had gone through that. But I couldn't stand them showing up late for gigs and nodding off on the bandstand. I couldn't tolerate that."

Miles actually fired John Coltrane—the greatest saxophone player since Charlie Parker—from his band. That was the sweetest gift he could have given him. Coltrane was forced to get his act together. Like Miles, he quit heroin cold turkey. And now, like Miles, his music was thriving. But they were both incredibly strong. For every Miles and Coltrane, there were a dozen other jazzmen who had lost everything—their music, their loved ones, their lives—because of heroin.

"Yow."

Viper heard the piercing sound at his feet. He looked down to see the one four-legged creature at the Cathouse that dared to come close to him. She had shiny beige fur that resembled cashmere, and sparkling green eyes. She looked straight up at the Viper and greeted him again.

"*Yow.*"

Yes, Viper thought, if Yolanda DeVray were transformed into a cat, this is what she would look like. The honey-toned, emerald-eyed cat rubbed its neck against Viper's ankle. His nose started quivering. Viper had just enough time to pull a handkerchief from his breast pocket before letting go a torrential sneeze.

"Achoooooo!"

The Yolanda-cat scurried away.

"God bless you, Viper," a chorus of jazzmen said.

Viper heard a telephone ring in the distance.

"*Gesundheit, liebe Viper,*" the baroness said in a perfect German accent as she walked past him, on the way to her bedroom. Nica nimbly tiptoed through the writhing carpet of cats lounging between the bedroom door and the rattling telephone on the nightstand. She picked up on the fifth ring.

"Good evening."

"Baroness? This is Detective Red Carney."

"What can I do for you, Red?"

"I'm going to ask you this question once. And do not lie. Is the Viper at your house?"

"Yes."

"Put him on the line."

* * *

"I am your master of ceremonies," Peewee crowed into the microphone onstage. "Welcome to the slammingest, jammingest, bebop bammingest joint uptown. I know it's cool to party with the white folks on 52nd Street, I dig that scene too, but if you really wants to get down, you gots to be uptown. So welcome to *my* house! It's Peewee's, y'all!"

By the fall of 1948, Peewee's had indeed become the hippest club in Harlem, rivaled only by Minton's Playhouse. And just as the partners at Mr. O's law firm, Schneider, Miller, and Bloom, had predicted, the demand for marijuana was expanding. The deliveries from the California pot farm arrived every two weeks, and Viper Morton managed a network of dealers out of the business manager's office in the back of Peewee's.

As for the man who gave his name to the club, Peewee had been furious when he found out three years earlier that the stay-at-home wife Pretty Paul Baxter was always braggin' about was, in fact, Yolanda DeVray.

"That bitch never once sought me out," he had fumed to Viper. "Not you or Pork Chop neither, to thank us for savin' her life! Instead, she sneaks back into town with her high yella faggot husband. Fuck these fucking inbred Creoles!"

Peewee was so angry, he married his Greenwich Village girlfriend, a blond-haired, blue-eyed heiress named Sally Anne Whitman. At least, she was an heiress when he married her. Once her parents learned she had eloped with a Negro, Sally was promptly disinherited. She was a Bohemian, an abstract expressionist painter. She and Peewee bought a loft and quickly produced two beautiful little kids.

"When are *you* gonna settle down, Clyde?" Pork Chop asked on a regular basis.

Viper's oldest friend in Harlem was the leader of the house band at the club. And he had finally found a wife. It was Athena Carson, who ran Lady Athena's, one of the top beauty parlors in Harlem. She and Pork Chop had known each other for years. He was godfather to the two children she'd had with Pork Chop's close buddy Dick Carson. Dick was in a black combat unit, died in action in Germany in the final weeks of the war. Pork Chop comforted Lady Athena, then wound up marrying her. She was a regular at the club.

"You lookin' real good tonight, Lady Athena," Peewee called out from the stage on this October night. "You better tell Pork Chop to watch out!"

"Yeah, Peewee," Athena shot back from her table on the nightclub floor. "You short men is always long on talk, ain't you?"

The crowd roared with laughter.

"All right, ladies and gentlemen," the pint-sized emcee announced, "let me introduce one of our regular acts here at Peewee's: we love him, we hate him, all you women want him, and so do half the men; and as for what he wants, well, name your price—I give you Pretty Paul Baxter!"

The ginger-toned baritone bounded onto the stage and launched into a high-speed scat, Pork Chop and the house band backing him with bebop brio.

Pretty Paul was not only one of the most popular singers at the club. As a marijuana dealer, he was one of Viper's biggest earners. Before his performance that night, as the club was opening for business, Paul had stepped into Viper's office and handed him a document-sized envelope stuffed with cash.

"Here you go, boss, this weekend's take."

"Thanks, Paul. How you been?"

"I'm in a good groove, Viper. I'm headlining on 52nd Street next week, at the Onyx."

"I'll be there. You heard about Bill Henry?"

"Yeah, that's a cryin' shame. But you know I don't shoot up anymore, Viper. Look!" Pretty Paul rolled up his sleeves, showed his veins. "I've been clean for a year. Yolanda finally got me to quit."

"How's she doin'?" Viper asked, trying to sound less curious than he felt. "Nobody ever sees her. Except Lady Athena, when she goes to the beauty parlor."

"Yolanda's all right. She's just a homebody."

"Give her my best. Paul, you say you aren't shooting heroin. That's good. But I don't allow anyone working for me to be *dealing* heroin."

"I ain't dealin' junk, Viper."

"I hope that's true, Paul. 'Cause if you are, there will be consequences."

"Trust me, Viper," Paul said, flashing his starry grin. "Trust me."

*　　*　　*

Heroin was spreading wider and faster. Buttercup Jones's whorehouse had become a major center of distribution. Things had got so bad that Viper, Peewee, and Pork Chop organized a sit-down with Buttercup at five o'clock one Monday morning, at the breakfast party at Hutch's Hideaway.

"I feel like you gentlemen are urging me to bankrupt myself," Buttercup said, nibbling on a thin slice of crispy bacon. Flamboyant as ever, he wore a finely tailored pin-striped suit and a silk turban.

"Lemme explain, Buttercup," Pork Chop said. "You were a dancer before you became a pimp and a drug dealer. I'm a musician. And I love reefer just about as much as I love makin' music. But I don't love it *more* than I love makin' music. Jazz and marijuana evolved together, they go hand in hand. Heroin ain't like reefer, Buttercup."

"Is that right?" Buttercup said. "You don't like bebop, Pork Chop?"

"I love it. I play it. And I hire beboppers to play in Peewee's house band. But they're missin' gigs. They're disappearing for days. They're selling their instruments. Why? Because they come to love junk *more* than they love makin' music. I don't know how many of his clarinets Bill Henry pawned for a fix. Finally, he wasn't makin' music at all. He lived for junk. And died in the gutter."

"Now come on, Pork Chop, Viper, Peewee, you know as much as I do, this is all about supply and demand. Musicians demand junk, somebody's gonna supply it to them. If it ain't me, it'll be somebody else."

"Why can't you just sell your Mexican locoweed?" Peewee asked.

"Because everybody prefers your California grass!" Buttercup said. "You bastards are putting me out of the reefer business and tellin' me now to get out of the heroin business."

"What about your whorehouse?" Peewee challenged. "You must be makin' money from that."

"Yeah, some, but I haven't seen any of you there lately. At least Pork Chop and Peewee are married. What's your excuse, Viper?"

"Buttercup," Viper said, "we're here to talk business."

"Good, then let's talk business. Who do you think is supplying me?" They knew the answer, but Buttercup paused for effect: "I'm backed up by the Sicilian Mafia."

"Meaning what?" Viper said.

"Meaning I ain't scared of you niggas," Buttercup hissed. "As long as there are junkies in Harlem, I'm gonna be sellin' 'em junk."

"Charlie Parker is a wreck," Pork Chop said. "Fats Navarro just wound up in the hospital again. Slim Jackson is at death's door. Junk is killin' jazz by killin' off its artists."

"I'm a drug dealer!" Buttercup said. "Just like you motherfuckers. Heroin is a booming business. Rather than trying to fight me, if you niggas had any capitalist sense at all, you'd be joinin' me."

"Well, we're not joining you," Viper said. "And we won't try to put you out of business. But we employ a network of dealers who understand that we don't approve of sellin' junk. If we find out that anyone who's dealin' weed for us is also dealin' junk for you, we're gonna consider that a conflict of interest. And we're gonna hold you responsible for instigating it. And we're gonna come around to inflict a penalty."

"I invite you boys to come around anytime," Buttercup said evenly. "I'll be waiting for you."

* * *

Viper felt a twinge of bitter satisfaction as he entered the Onyx, one of the hippest of the 52nd Street jazz clubs, and saw that the place was less than full. Pretty Paul Baxter and His Orchestra were headlining tonight. Viper walked in the door just as the first set was ending. He spotted Yolanda sitting alone at a table for four, sipping a Coca-Cola.

"Clyyyyde." Yolanda said his name liltingly, lovingly. "I hoped I would see you here tonight. Join me, please."

"Yo-Yo," he said, taking the seat directly across the small round table from her, "this is the first time I've seen you in a club since . . . since . . ."

"The Savoy. The night of my twenty-first birthday. I think of it often. That was almost seven years ago."

"So Pretty Paul let you out of the house for some special reason?"

"As a matter of fact, we're celebrating. Don't tell anybody, but I'm pregnant."

Viper felt a catch in his throat. "Congratulations, Yo-Yo."

"We've been trying for three years. Paul was starting to give up on me."

"What a guy."

"Don't start, Clyde. Can I ask you a question? You've been back from the war for three years, you're makin' good money. Why haven't you gotten married?"

"Maybe I'm waiting for you."

They stared hard into each other's eyes. Viper wanted to kiss her. He felt that if he leaned over the table and dared, she would let him.

"Well, look who's decided to grace us with his presence!" Pretty Paul shouted as he walked up to the table. He slapped Viper on the back. "Too bad you missed the first set, man." Paul sat down, gave Yolanda a big, noisy kiss on the cheek. "How's my girl?"

"I'm fine, Daddy," Yolanda said coquettishly.

Paul gestured to a posh-looking white man to take the last seat at the table. "Viper, meet Rémy Arnaud, straight off a plane from Paris, France."

"Good evening, sir," Arnaud said. "You are the famous Viper Morton?"

"You've heard of me?"

"I own a jazz club in Paris, the neighborhood of Saint-Germain. Many American jazz musicians are coming to play at my club. They all speak of you."

"Rémy's tryin' to get me to come to Paris," Paul said.

"With your lovely wife, of course," Arnaud said.

"That would be a dream!" Yolanda said. "I've never been to France. You know, Rémy, my maiden name is DeVray."

"So you are a true Frenchwoman, then?"

"Paul and I are both Creole, from New Orleans."

"Yolanda ain't going nowhere," Paul said. "She's gonna stay in Harlem and raise our kids. But, shit, I'll come to gay Paree for a few weeks."

"You are already known there," Rémy Arnaud said. "For your last record, with the handsome photo. The French ladies, they love your face."

"Yeah, I know. I work on my voice. But my face is my fortune."

"I've got to go," Viper said, rising from the table.

"Ain't you even gonna stay for the second set?" Paul said.

"I got to make the rounds of all the clubs on Fifty-Second tonight, Paul. I got my own personal clients to take care of. You know that."

"Good night, Mr. Viper Morton," Arnaud said. "It was a pleasure to meet you."

"Good night, Clyde," Yolanda said.

"Good night, Yo-Yo."

* * *

Viper was sitting in his office on a quiet afternoon, counting stacks of money, when the rattling phone broke his concentration.

"Yeah?" he said.

"Clyde? Can you meet me?"

"Yo-Yo. Are you all right?" It had been two weeks since he'd seen her at the Onyx. "Where are you?"

"I'm in a phone booth. Do you remember where we went for that walk, in Riverside Park? Can you meet me there in fifteen minutes?"

Viper found Yolanda sitting on the bench where he had held her close three years earlier. She wore a head scarf and large sunglasses. As he sat down beside her, she removed the glasses. Viper gasped. Yolanda's left eye was swollen shut, bruised blue.

"Paul threw a fit, Clyde. I had another miscarriage. I told him about my abortion. He said I was damaged goods. Then he started beating me."

"Where is he now?"

"He stormed out while I was lying on the floor. I don't know where he went. But I was too scared to stay in the house. Scared he might come back."

"Don't go home. Go to Lady Athena's beauty parlor. She and Pork Chop can give you a room. Wait there until I come see you."

"There's something else, Clyde. Paul's been dealing heroin for Buttercup."

"Since when?"

"Since forever. He's never stopped. I just thought you should know."

"Thanks, Yo-Yo. Now get over to Athena's. I'll find Pretty Paul."

"Don't hurt him, Clyde. Please don't hurt him."

Viper headed first to the club, to talk to Peewee and Pork Chop. They knew where to find Pretty Paul on a weekday afternoon. He was at the pool hall down the street from Peewee's.

"What you fellas want with me?" Paul asked, setting down his pool cue as the three of them walked in.

"Come with us, Paul," Viper said. "We need to talk with you at the club."

They took Pretty Paul to the rooftop of Peewee's.

"You guys seem upset about something," Paul said. "Yolanda's my wife, y'all. I can treat her any damn way I please."

"Yeah, and you our employee," Peewee said. "And we gonna hang you like the laundry."

"What, huh?"

Peewee took hold of Pretty Paul's left leg. Pork Chop gripped him by the right. They suspended him, upside down, over the ledge of the rooftop. His arms flailed in the air.

"Please don't kill me!" Pretty Paul screamed, hysterical, hanging upside down, six floors up from the pavement. "Don't kill me!"

"You beat your wife, Paul," Pork Chop said. "We don't approve."

"I won't do it again!" Paul shrieked. "I promise!"

"Don't make us drop you, Paul!" Peewee said with a malevolent giggle.

"Don't drop me! Please don't drop me!" Paul's arms windmilled helplessly in the air.

"You dealin' junk for Buttercup?" Viper said.

"Yes! But I'll stop, I promise!"

"How much money you made dealin' for Buttercup?"

"I don't know!"

"Oops!" Peewee said, letting go of Paul's leg.

"Don't drop me!" Paul cried. "Please don't drop me! Ten thousand dollars. I made ten grand dealin' junk for Buttercup."

"Okay," Viper said, "pull him up."

Pork Chop and Peewee lifted Paul and put him back on his feet. He was convulsing like a jackhammer.

"I'm sorry, fellas," Paul said, his voice trembling. "Please forgive me."

"Paul," Viper said, "take us to Buttercup."

*   *   *

Everybody knew the location of his whorehouse on 112th Street, but few people knew where Buttercup Jones actually lived. Pretty Paul, still rattled after his hang from the rooftop, took Viper and Peewee to Buttercup's private lair, a posh townhouse in the Morningside Heights area of Harlem. The pimp and heroin dealer greeted them when they rang the doorbell. He wore a leopard print bathrobe over dark blue silk pajamas. His feet were in embroidered slippers, and his hair in curlers.

"Welcome, boys," Buttercup said, almost as if he had been expecting them. "Come into the salon."

Buttercup led them into a dimly lit room. He sat down on a small couch and gestured to his guests to sit in three elegant, French-looking chairs. Paul sat down, but Viper and Peewee stayed on their feet.

"Let's talk business," Buttercup said.

"Pretty Paul tells us he's sold ten grand worth of junk for you," Viper said.

"Paul's a natural born salesman," Buttercup said with a smirk. "You fellas know that."

"We told you that if there was a conflict of interest, we would inflict a penalty."

"We're here to collect," Peewee said.

"By our measure," Viper said, "you owe us ten grand."

"I'm sorry, Buttercup," Paul said, clutching the arms of his chair, still trying to calm himself. "These motherfuckers is crazy."

"No worries, Paul. Viper, Peewee, if that's the price, I'm happy to pay it. I've got ten thousand dollars under this couch cushion."

"Pay up," Peewee said.

Buttercup rose, reached under the cushion, and whipped out a machete.

"Die, motherfuckers!" Buttercup screamed, spinning around and brandishing the weapon above his head. He swung the machete at Peewee. The little man ducked. Buttercup missed Peewee but slashed open Pretty Paul's left cheek. Blood geysered.

"My face!" Paul shrieked. "My face!"

Viper crouched as Buttercup moved toward him, swinging the machete. "Die, motherfuckers!" he screamed again.

Peewee pulled a pistol out of his jacket pocket and—

Blam! Blam! Blam!

—blasted Buttercup with three shots. The pimp fell backward, sprawled on his couch, eyes wide open, his chest gushing blood. Meanwhile Pretty Paul writhed on the floor, clutching his bubbling gash.

"Aaaarrrrrggggh! My face! My face!"

"Shut the fuck up!" Peewee shouted.

Blam!

Peewee shot Paul once in the head, right in the center of his right temple.

The dimly lit room was suddenly deathly quiet. The acrid smell of gun smoke filled the air.

"Damn, Peewee," Viper said. "What we gonna do now?"

Peewee grabbed Paul's right hand, placed his pistol in it, twisted Paul's finger around the trigger.

"We gonna get the fuck outta here."

* * *

One hour later, Viper went to see Yolanda. Lady Athena had given her a room above the beauty parlor.

"Clyde, what's happened?"

"I have some bad news, Yo-Yo. I just talked to Detective Red Carney. He says Paul and Buttercup had a fight. Buttercup attacked Paul with a machete. Paul whipped out a gun, shot Buttercup three times, and then, in a panic, I guess . . . shot himself in the head."

Yolanda looked stricken. "Paul's dead?"

"I'm sorry, Yo-Yo."

"But Paul never owned a gun."

"Not that you knew of."

"Good Lord."

Yo-Yo threw her arms around Viper.

"Hold me, Clyde. Please hold me."

Viper squeezed Yolanda against his body, the warmth and softness and sweet smell of her arousing him. He desperately wanted to make love to her. But he knew this wasn't the time.

"The police are looking for you," Viper whispered in Yolanda's ear. "You should go to Red Carney's office right away."

"Thank you, Clyde," Yolanda said, fighting back tears. "Thank you."

*   *   *

Saint Peter's in Harlem had a reputation as the place where jazz people went to worship. And to mourn. The church was jam-packed for the memorial service—one week after their untimely deaths—for Pretty Paul Baxter and Buttercup Jones. Viper sat in the front pew. On one side of him were Pork Chop and Lady Athena. They stared straight ahead, with solemn expressions. On the other side of Viper sat Peewee. The little killer kept tossing his head and rolling his eyes as the preacher frequently seemed to address his sermon directly to him and his partners.

"Crime does not pay, my brothers and sisters!" the white-haired minister thundered. "Pretty Paul Baxter was a talented singer. Buttercup Jones was a gifted dancer. But they gave in to a life of crime!" The preacher pulled out a handkerchief and mopped the sweat pouring down his face. He'd been going on for some time now and seemed to be building to a crescendo. "Pimpin'. Gamblin'. Dealin' narcotics. Paul and Buttercup succumbed to the criminal life. And in the end, they were literally at each other's throats. 'Cause that's what a life of crime does to a man!"

Everyone who was anyone in the jazz world was at Saint Peter's that day. Viper had even spotted Rémy Arnaud in the crowd, the Frenchman who owned a jazz club in Paris. Everyone was there, that is, except Pretty Paul's widow. Viper tried not to be too obvious about it, but he kept turning his head, trying to get a glimpse of Yo-Yo. She was nowhere to be seen.

"Dear Lord," the preacher intoned, "please forgive Pretty Paul and Buttercup for their sins. Let them embrace each other in the kingdom of heaven."

Peewee leaned over to Viper and said, almost loud enough for the preacher to hear, "Let them suck each other's dicks in hell."

"Though there be criminals amongst us still," the preacher boomed, glowering down from the pulpit at the criminals in the front row, "even here in this holy place, please dear Lord, let them see the light! Before they too end up like Paul Baxter, who has left behind a grieving widow." Now the preacher's voice turned hoarse with pity. "Still so young, still so beautiful, and now abandoned, alone, so all alone. My brothers and sisters, Yolanda DeVray Baxter has agreed to sing a song today in memory of her husband."

Yolanda emerged from a door behind the altar. She wore a black dress and black sunglasses. The crowd was utterly silent as she walked up to the pulpit. The preacher stepped away, gesturing for her to take his place. Yolanda stood perfectly still for a long moment. Then, she opened her mouth to sing . . .

Yolanda's voice went straight to your heart. Pierced it, caressed it, broke it apart, then gently healed it. Viper remembered the night in 1941 when she'd won first prize at the Apollo Theater Amateur Night competition. That was the only other time he'd heard Yo-Yo sing. She still had the voice of a fierce angel. But today, seven years later, there was a new, shattering aspect: this was a voice suffused with pain. During her song at the Apollo, seven years ago, Yo-Yo had stared at Viper the whole time. Now, in the church pulpit, her eyes concealed behind the black sunglasses, it was impossible to know who or what she was looking at as she sang. As Yolanda hit the final note of her song, the crowd in the church rose as one and exploded in applause. Yolanda's face remained impassive, stoical, inscrutable. She descended from the altar, then walked alone down the aisle as the church full of jazz people applauded her, tears in their eyes. She walked right past them all, straight out the church door.

From the pulpit the preacher hollered: "Amen! Amen! Amen, my brothers and sisters! Let the congregation cry amen!"

The multitude of voices roared in response: *"Amen!"*

* * *

After the service, Viper returned to his apartment and lay on the couch. He didn't know what to do with himself. A week ago this day, he had gone to see Yolanda to tell her that her husband was dead. He'd concealed his role in what had happened. Led her to believe that it was Red Carney who had described the scene of the crime to him. Since then, Viper had deliberately stayed away from Yolanda. He wanted to give her time and space to deal with the aftermath of this tragedy; deal with her family and Pretty Paul's; deal with the police investigation. Viper didn't want to crowd her, didn't want to demand her attention. He had no idea what Yo-Yo planned to do. If she would stay in New York or return to New Orleans. Or if, after all these years, she would finally belong to him. To *him*. Not to Mr. O. Not to Pretty Paul. But to him, and him alone.

The doorbell rang. Viper spied Yolanda through the peephole, swung open the door.

"Hello, Clyde."

"Come in, Yolanda."

She took off her sunglasses. Even with heavy makeup, there was still a blue circle around her left eye.

"Sorry to just show up like this."

"I knew you'd come. Sit down. A drink?"

"Sure. Bourbon, on the rocks."

"You sang beautifully today, Yo-Yo."

"Thank you, Clyde. I'm still sort of in shock."

"That's understandable."

He prepared two glasses of Wild Turkey with ice, then sat beside her on the couch.

"I keep running the story through my mind," Yolanda said. "I can see how Buttercup and Paul would have had a fight. I can even accept that Paul had a gun and would have shot Buttercup. But one thing still doesn't make sense to me: Why would Paul then shoot himself in the head?"

"Buttercup had sliced open Paul's face with a machete," Viper said. "You heard Paul say it yourself: his face was his fortune. I think it was a sudden tragic reaction to what had just happened."

"I don't know, Clyde. I never took Paul for someone who would commit suicide."

"I know what you feel, Yo-Yo." Viper paused and took a long sip of his drink, to brace himself, before he continued. "Can I tell you something? Something I've never told anyone before. Back in Alabama, I had a fiancée. I left her when we were both nineteen years old. I came up to New York to try to make it as a trumpet player. Bertha was devastated. She was pregnant. I acted like I didn't know. But I knew. I left her, all the same. Only two years later did I learn that soon after I left, Bertha killed herself."

"Oh, no! Good Lord!"

"She slit her throat with a straight razor."

"Oh, Clyde! How awful!"

"I didn't take Bertha for someone who would commit suicide. Just as you didn't see Paul that way. But I know what you're going through, Yo-Yo. I want you to know that I'm here for you."

"Thank you, Clyde."

They fell silent. Sipped their drinks. Finally, Viper spoke.

"So what are you going to do now? Are you going to do what you were born to do? Are you going to become a singer?"

"Yes, Clyde, I finally am."

"Do you remember that night you sang at the Apollo? You asked me if I would be your manager. Well, I would love to do that for you, if you still want me."

"Oh, Clyde. No one has been as kind to me, as protective of me as you."

"I've waited many years for this chance, Yolanda. You told me long ago that I was the one you really wanted. Is it finally our time?"

"That's what I've come here to tell you, Clyde. I'm moving to Paris."

"What?"

"I talked to Rémy Arnaud. The Frenchman. He's asked me to come sing at his club in Saint Germain. To be a permanent act there. I'm leaving tomorrow."

"Paris?" Viper nearly spat out the word. He could feel a rage come over him, like a sudden fever. "You gonna go live in Paris? And what about us?"

"You can come visit."

"Come visit? I thought you wanted to be with me. I thought I was the one you wanted. Was that just a lie?"

"Clyde, Paris could be my big break. The chance I missed out on."

Viper was yelling now. "Yeah, and where the hell is your gratitude? How many times do I have to save your miserable fucking life? This is how you repay me?"

"Repay you?"

He rose from the couch, the words exploding from him. "Get out! Get the fuck outta my house!"

"Clyde, please!"

"Get out! I don't ever want to see you again!"

Yolanda left in a hurry, slamming the door behind her.

Viper flung himself on the couch and wept. Cried his eyes out. Like a woman, he thought bitterly. He even cried himself to sleep.

In the morning, he woke up and made a decision. Viper had told Yolanda about Bertha. What he hadn't told her was that he hardly ever thought of Bertha. It was as if he had placed all memories of his dead fiancée in a drawer. A drawer he'd locked and almost never opened. Now, he would do the same with all his memories of Yo-Yo. He would forget Yolanda DeVray had ever existed.

* * *

"Achooo!" Viper unleashed another mighty sneeze.

"God bless you, Viper," a bunch of jazzmen said.

Viper gave a little nod of thanks as he wiped his nose with his handkerchief. He glanced at his Rolex. It was one thirty on this November night in 1961, the night of the Viper's third murder. So far, I've only told you about his first, the night he slit West Indian Charlie's throat in

1940. Back in 1948, it was Peewee, as you know, not Viper, who killed Pretty Paul Baxter and Buttercup Jones. Viper's second and third murders came a little more than a year apart. His second killing, last year, had dark repercussions. Still, he did not regret what he had done in 1960.

But tonight. What he had done tonight had staggered him. Maybe Pork Chop was right. Maybe he was still in shock. Viper felt his eyes starting to water.

"Viper, are you all right?"

He looked up and saw the baroness standing over him. "Yes, Nica," he said, fighting back tears. "I'm just allergic to your cats."

Nica leaned down and whispered in his ear. "There's a call for you, Viper. It's Red Carney."

The baroness led Viper to her bedroom, handed him the telephone from the nightstand, then turned and left him alone with the cats.

"Carney?"

"Viper, what the hell did I tell you?"

"That I had three hours to disappear."

"That was two and a half hours ago. You think because I'm a New York cop I can't come over to New Jersey and arrest your black ass? After all you've been up to the past twenty-five years, you're a fucking federal case, Viper. The FBI would give me a medal for bringing you in."

"So, what are you waiting for, Red?"

He heard the rogue cop sigh over the telephone line.

"All right, Viper. If that's the way you want to play it. You're better off surrendering to me than to anybody else."

"Surrender," Viper said solemnly. "Don't know if I like that word."

"Well, you've got thirty minutes to change your mind," Carney said. "Otherwise, meet me outside of the Cathouse at two o'clock."

"All right."

"And Viper . . ."

"What?"

"Don't make me kill you."

8

By the age of thirty-seven, Clyde "the Viper" Morton had become a very wealthy man. Since the day Yolanda DeVray left for Paris, nearly seven years earlier, Viper had thrown himself maniacally into his work. He now owned *two* Cadillacs, one silver, one black. He moved into a grand apartment on Harlem's Sugar Hill. His neighbors were the black elite: surgeons and college professors, lawyers and politicians, prominent ministers and entrepreneurs, celebrity athletes and entertainers. His art deco building on Edgecombe Avenue had a uniformed black doorman (just like Mr. O's place on Park Avenue), a sprawling marble lobby, and a uniformed black elevator man (just like Mr. O's). Viper didn't live in a penthouse, but his fifth-floor domain at the summit of Harlem gave him a sweeping view of Northern Manhattan. Like the folks said: "Life is sweet on Sugar Hill!"

He began dabbling in Harlem real estate. With the support of the law firm Schneider, Miller, and Bloom, he'd bought his old brownstone on Lenox Avenue from its longtime realtors. He rented out eleven of the twelve apartments and kept his old place as a second residence for himself. It felt good to own a building. But Viper knew that he was still a modest player in the real estate game.

Something called "urban renewal" had come to Harlem. Take what had happened to the vast wasteland of rusting metal once known as One-Eyed Willie's Junkyard. The final resting place, if you will, of Mr. O, became the terrain for one of the housing projects popping up all over the capital of Black America. In what was a typical deal, the local and federal governments paid Wieseltier & Sons Development Corporation public funds to build a complex of massive concrete towers: a dozen twenty-story-high, anonymous-looking edifices that were given (perhaps ironically?) the name Renaissance Gardens. After construction was complete, Wieseltier repaid the government its investment by buying the "public housing" complex from it. The real estate company then condemned several blocks of old Harlem tenements it owned, six-story structures festooned with fire escapes, populated by families that had lived in the neighborhood for generations. The tenements might have been turning decrepit, but they had character. Neighbors sat and chatted on the front stoops, and little kids played on the sidewalk in front of the buildings, under the watchful eyes of elders who were linked to them not by blood, but by a shared sense of community. But once those tenements were doomed to the wrecking ball, all those residents were dispatched to Renaissance Gardens, where their rents were jacked up for the privilege of living in such modernity. Wieseltier & Sons then tore down the blocks of tenements and replaced them with yet more identically anonymous housing projects, stacking more floors of black families high into the sky.

The urban renewers made piles of money. And they said that what they were doing was for the public good, providing desperately needed lodging for the exploding Harlem population of low-income families. While their builders argued that the concrete towers were a triumph of mid-century architectural design, projects like Renaissance Gardens often gave Viper a quiet shiver when he drove past them in one of his Cadillacs. Whatever the Wieseltiers and other renewers said about the projects, he knew that they had to know what the buildings resembled. They looked like prisons. And prison was the one thing Viper dreaded more than death.

Folks would have been surprised to hear that Viper Morton bore any secret dreads. In Harlem, fear of the Viper had returned. It was widely believed that Viper had killed Pretty Paul Baxter and Buttercup Jones for dealing heroin and that, before he shot him in the head, he had sliced open Paul's beautiful face out of sheer badness. In high Machiavellian style, fear was the ultimate respect.

And perhaps an aphrodisiac. Still a bachelor, Viper didn't lack for female companionship. In the course of any given year, he bedded more women than he could name. And he hadn't loved any of them.

Once or twice a year, Viper received a letter from Yolanda DeVray, postmarked "Paris, France." Viper tossed every letter in the trash, never opening a single envelope, never reading a single word of what Yo-Yo had wanted to say to him.

Viper thrived. But in bitterness.

*   *   *

While his headquarters remained in Harlem, Viper was spending more and more time in midtown, on what most jazzmen had simply started calling "the Street." The neon-bathed stretch of 52nd Street between Fifth and Sixth Avenues was now firmly established as the center of the jazz universe. Strolling past the Club Downbeat, Jimmy Ryan's, the Famous Door, Viper sometimes felt a twinge of melancholy. When he had arrived in New York nearly two decades earlier, white folks had to come up to Harlem, to *our* turf, to hear the most exciting music in the world. Now, black artists had to bring the music down to the white man's domain. It didn't make the music any less great. But Viper couldn't help but feel that somehow Harlem—as with the destruction of the tenements and the construction of the projects—had lost something precious it would never get back.

Late one night in February 1955, Viper dropped by one of the hottest spots on the Street: Birdland, the club named after Charlie Parker, founding father of bebop. The club was packed, but Bird himself was nowhere to be seen. Art Blakey and the Jazz Messengers were onstage. Viper saw Dizzy Gillespie sitting at a table, surrounded by admirers, holding court. Diz wore his trademark beret and tortoiseshell glasses. He gave Viper a wink and a nod as the reefer man walked past. In the corner, Viper spotted Thelonious Monk, wearing a giant Siberian fur hat. Sitting next to him was an elegant white woman with long black hair, smoking a cigarette in a long black cigarette holder. She smiled and gestured for Viper to come over. Somehow, they had not yet met. But he knew who she was. The jazzmen had been talking about her arrival on the scene for months.

"You must be Viper Morton."

"And you must be the Baroness Rothschild."

"Rothschild was my maiden name. But please, call me Nica."

"Hey, Monk," Viper said.

"What's up, Viper?" Monk growled.

"Please sit, Viper," Nica said. "Have a drink with us."

Viper took a seat. "So you're actually living in New York now, not just visiting?"

"Exactly. I've taken a suite at the Stanhope Hotel. You should come by sometime. We have jams that go on all night."

"Excuse me, lady and gentleman," Monk said. He rose and walked toward the men's room.

"You're quite a figure in this town, Viper."

"Yes, and you're quickly becoming one, Nica. Cats are already writing songs named for you."

"Not long ago, I was leading the dreary life of a diplomat's wife. Then one day, someone put on a recording of "Round Midnight' by Thelonious Monk. I had what I guess you could call an epiphany. I knew I had to meet that composer. Then I discovered more of the music. And I knew I had to live in that world of musicians."

"A patron of the art," Viper said, making no effort to hide his skepticism.

"You and I aren't so different, Viper. You provide the jazzmen with something they need. And I help them when it comes to making the rent or paying a bill."

"Or scoring some junk?"

"No, Viper. I don't give them money for heroin. I want to help musicians to live. Not help them to die."

"Why don't you save me, Diz?"

A howl of indescribable anguish echoed through the club.

"*Why don't you save me?*"

The music abruptly stopped. All heads turned to Dizzy Gillespie's table. Charlie Parker stood looming over the table, looking like a bum who had just wandered in from the street. He was wild-eyed, wearing a ratty old raincoat, wailing at his former bandmate.

"*Why don't you save me, Diz? Why don't you save me?*"

It was obvious that Bird was out of his mind on junk. Dizzy stared at his friend helplessly.

"*Save me, Diz! Please save me!*"

Two bouncers appeared and grabbed Charlie Parker by the arms.

"*Save me, Diz!*"

Bird wailed and flailed as he was dragged out of the nightclub that had been named in his honor.

"*Please save me!*"

That was when everyone knew. It would only be a matter of time now.

*   *   *

"*News flash!*" the announcer intoned over the radio in Viper's office. "*Bebop king dies in baroness's flat! Charlie 'Yardbird' Parker, the Negro saxophonist known for starting the bop jazz craze, was found dead in the Stanhope Hotel suite of a luscious, creamy-skinned, raven-haired European heiress of the Rothschild fortune. The authorities say no drugs were found on the premises. But they consider the death to be drug related.*"

Viper summoned Peewee and Pork Chop to an emergency meeting on the rooftop of Peewee's club.

"This is the worst thing that coulda happened," Pork Chop said. "Now Bird's a martyr. And all the young cats

are gonna wanna shoot up to show that they're misunder-
stood geniuses, too. Just like Bird."

"Like they didn't mimic him enough when he was
alive," Viper said. "You know what I'm thinkin'? We
should take out more heroin dealers."

"We can't do that," Peewee said. "Most of them are
backed by the Mafia. The I-talians might suspect it was us
that got rid of Buttercup, and they mighta let us get away
with it. But that was seven years ago. There's a lot more
money at stake today."

"All we can do is vow to keep resisting," Pork Chop said.

"Yeah, I guess," Peewee said. "But sometimes I think
Buttercup was right. Junk is in demand. If we were serious
businessmen, we'd just go ahead and supply it."

"You can't start thinking that way, Peewee," Viper said.
"This is about something more important than money."

"Yeah, I know. I'm just sayin' . . ."

"Pork Chop is right. We gotta keep resisting."

Viper held out his hand. Pork Chop grasped it.

"All for one and one for all," Pork Chop said.

"What are we now, the Three Musketeers?" Peewee
said with a snort. All the same, he placed his hand on top
of Viper's and Pork Chop's.

"Damn straight," Viper said. "United against heroin.
Till the day we die."

*   *   *

One summer night in 1958, after all his colleagues had
gone home, Dan Miller of the firm of Schneider, Miller,
and Bloom invited Viper Morton to visit his office on Mad-
ison Avenue. The gaunt, young lawyer Viper first met in
1945 had turned into a paunchy, golf-playing suburbanite

on the threshold of middle age, satisfied with himself as
a successful husband, father, provider . . . and high-class
drug trafficker. Miller broke out whiskey and cigars. He
then spent a good half hour praising Viper's management
of the ever-expanding marijuana business before getting to
the point of the meeting. "Viper, we're opening a nightclub
in Los Angeles. We're going to call it Peewee's West."

"Does Peewee know?"

"Not yet. But he'll have little to do with it. The firm
has a trademark on his name, as a brand. You, on the other
hand, will start spending two weeks a month in L.A., to
help our colleagues out there get a gage enterprise running
from inside the club."

"Well, thank you, Dan."

"You'll basically be an elder statesman. We think we
have a solid team in place, but we want you there to mentor them in the first couple of years of operations."

"Sounds promising."

"We plan to fly you out to L.A. next week. But of
course we'll need to have someone help handle your duties
here in New York. We have a young fellow in mind. He's
been working in our Kansas City operation. Goes by the
name of Randall 'Country' Johnson."

"Country?" Viper said mockingly. "If folks in Kansas
City call him 'Country,' he must be a real hick."

"Maybe. But he's a fast learner. Twenty-one years old.
A young man of promise. And he can provide muscle when
we need it. He's smart, charming, and brutal."

"And you think he's ready for New York?"

"That will be for you to decide, Viper. He arrives in
town tonight. I suggest you meet him tomorrow for a . . .
what to call it?"

"A job interview."

"Exactly."

*   *   *

At eleven o'clock the next morning, Viper and Peewee greeted the interviewee in the kitchen of the Harlem nightclub.

"It sho is a honor for me to meet you, Mr. Viper, Mr. Peewee," Country said. He was tall and rangy, with a loping gait and an eager, gap-toothed grin. He wore a boxy brown suit, a wide paisley tie, and two-toned shoes.

"So this is your first time in New York, Country?" Peewee asked.

"My first time up North a-tall, Mr. Peewee."

"All right, Country," Viper said, "let me get straight to our most serious problem."

"Yessir, Mr. Viper."

"Heroin just gets more and more popular. But we do not sell junk. Now, I hear you're an ambitious young man. What reason do we have to believe that you might not decide to start selling heroin, or allowing our gage dealers to do so?"

"Well, Mr. Viper," Country said, with an air of humble sincerity, "all I can do is give you my word."

"Yeah, that's the question, nigga," Peewee said. "Why should we take your word?"

Country looked down at the kitchen floor, paused, seemed to gather his emotions, then looked up again and said: "Well, Mr. Peewee, Mr. Viper . . . my Daddy, when he come home from the war, he had some real bad injuries. Seemed the only thing that would take his pain away was the morphine. So he started spendin' all the family money on morphine. Then, he started stealin' it. He become a addict. And he overdosed. I found him dead in the bathtub one morning. And so I was left to raise the family. To support my Mama and the three chil'run younger than me. I was fourteen. So far as I can see, heroin even worse than morphine. So I hate that shit, yessir, I hate it."

At that moment, Pork Chop entered the kitchen with a drummer called Sticks Anderson.

"Hey, fellas," Sticks said. Everybody liked Sticks. Fiftyish, short, round, and balding, he had an always amiable demeanor and a dreamy, not-all-there look in his eye. "Pork Chop come and grab me from rehearsal. What y'all want from me this morning?"

"Pork Chop," Viper said, "meet Country Johnson."

They shook hands. "Hello, young man," Pork Chop said.

"It's a honor, Mr. Pork Chop," Country said.

"Country," Viper said, "this is Sticks Anderson."

"Yeah, I know Sticks," Country said, his tone suddenly frosting over.

"Sure," Sticks said, still dreamy seeming. "We met in Kansas City once."

"You was on tour there. You a hell of a drummer, Mr. Sticks."

"And a miserable junkie," Peewee said.

"Which is *his* problem," Pork Chop said.

"*Our* problem," Viper said, "is that Sticks has been selling gage for us for years. And now, we learn he's been sellin' junk as well."

"Have a seat, Mr. Sticks," Country said frostily.

Sticks Anderson suddenly looked scared. He sat down at the table. "Now, I'll admit, I've sold a little junk now and then, fellas, but if you want me to stop, I will."

"Yeah, we gonna see to that, Mr. Sticks," Country said. "Thing about junk is you start to love shootin' up more than you love makin' music, ain't that so?"

"Look, fellas," Pork Chop interrupted, "Sticks said he'll stop."

"Thank you, Mr. Pork Chop," Country said. "I know you means well. But Mr. Sticks, you can't hold no drumsticks if you ain't got no thumbs, can you?"

Sticks furrowed his brow. "No thumbs?" he said, sounding perplexed.

"Prob'ly," Country said, "you be able to find somebody to stick a needle in your vein for you. But can't get nobody to play drums for you if you ain't got no thumbs."

"No thumbs?" Sticks asked again, frightened and confused. He looked to Viper, then to Peewee and Pork Chop, beseechingly. "What is this motherfucker talking about?"

"Hold him, Mr. Peewee!" Country ordered.

Peewee, small but strong, grabbed Sticks Anderson's left arm, twisted it behind his back. He grabbed Sticks's right arm at the wrist, held him down in the chair. Sticks looked terrified but put up little resistance. Country grabbed a meat cleaver from a hook on the kitchen wall.

"Hold his right hand flat on the table!" he ordered Peewee.

"Is this really necessary?" Pork Chop cried.

Peewee forced open Sticks's right hand, which had been balled up in a fist, pressed it down flat on the table.

Country raised the meat cleaver high above his head. "You love junk more than you love the drums, ain't that right, Mr. Sticks?" Country said.

Sticks wriggled in the chair, helpless under Peewee's grip. "Stop, no, please don't!"

And with one swift chop, Country cut off Sticks Anderson's right thumb. Blood shot out across the kitchen. Sticks screamed like an animal caught in a steel trap. "Aarrgghh!"

"Lay his other hand flat on the table!" Country yelled.

Peewee did as Country instructed him. Sticks Anderson, his right hand still gushing blood, stared in wide-eyed horror and disbelief as Peewee pressed down his left hand and Country raised high the cleaver once again.

"Stop!" Pork Chop screamed. "Don't do it!" He moved toward Country, but Viper grabbed him by the arm, holding him back.

"Please, no," Sticks begged. "Please don't!"

And with another swift, deadly accurate downward swoop, Country chopped off Sticks Anderson's other thumb. Another projectile stream of blood shot out across the kitchen.

Sticks fell to the floor, writhing in anguish, wailing. "Aaaaaarrrrrrrgggggghh!"

Country held up the two severed thumbs.

"Now, I'm gonna keep one of these for myself," he said calmly. "The other one I'm gonna give to Mr. Viper. And you let other motherfuckers who deal gage for us know what's gonna happen if they start dealin' junk."

"Oh, God, no!" Sticks wailed, rolling around on the floor, tucking his four-fingered hands under his arms, as if trying to hide them, to protect them from further harm.

Pork Chop grabbed two tablecloths from a shelf, wrapped them around Sticks's bloody hands.

"This was totally uncalled for!" Pork Chop said. "I'm takin' him to the hospital!"

Pork Chop and Sticks rushed from the kitchen.

Viper and Peewee stared at Country in astonishment. Country stared back at them expectantly.

The silence lingered. Until, finally . . .

"So, Mr. Viper," the young man asked, "how'd I do?"

"Country Johnson," Viper said, "you're hired."

*   *   *

That afternoon, Viper gave Country Johnson a tour in his silver Cadillac, showing him New York in the same way that Mr. O had had his chauffeur, Peewee, drive young Clyde Morton around Manhattan way back in 1936.

"This sho is nice of you, Mr. Viper. I know what a busy man you is." Country leaned out the window of the passenger seat and gawped at everything he saw: the Empire State Building, the Statue of Liberty, Times Square. Viper remembered the sense of wonder he'd felt upon seeing all this for the first time himself. "I growed up in Mississippi," Country said. "When I moved to Kansas City three years ago, that seemed like the biggest place in the world. But New York! Hot damn!"

"I can see why you came so highly recommended," Viper said. "I think you can go very far, Country."

"Well, that's real flatterin' comin' from you, Mr. Viper. You a legend down in Kansas City."

"Am I?"

"Yessir. Even some stone-cold gangsters respect you for not sellin' heroin. They know what you did to that West

Indian fella back in the day. And then Buttercup and Pretty Paul. Weren't so pretty when you got through with him."

"Now, I always heard it was the Mafia that killed Buttercup and Paul," Viper said.

Country let out a loud, goofy laugh. "Yeah, yeah, you don't got to say nothin' else, Mr. Viper. Everybody know you as discreet as you is lethal. Look what happened to that Jew gangster."

"Mr. O? Folks think I wasted Mr. O?"

Country laughed again and clapped his hands twice. "You don't got to say no more, Mr. Viper. Folks know that Jew gangster was the biggest gage dealer in New York. He disappeared and now you the biggest gage dealer in New York. Say no more, Mr. Viper. Just know that your name spells total respect."

"Well, thank you, Country. Let's head back up to Harlem. I'm taking you to my personal tailor, Seymour. He's an old man now, but he's still the best tailor in town. We're gonna get you dressed right. Then we're gonna swing by Gentleman Jack's barbershop so you can get a proper conk, a shave, and a manicure."

"A manicure? I thought that was only for faggots!"

"And successful businessmen, Country. I think you are going to be a very successful businessman."

"Why, thank you, Mr. Viper."

"Have you ever heard of Machiavelli?"

"He with the I-talian mob?"

"No, no. A Florentine philosopher from the sixteenth century."

"Sorry, Mr. Viper. I ain't real educated."

"Neither was I when I was your age, Country. Anyway, Machiavelli posed the question: Is it more important for a leader to be loved or feared? What do you say, Country?"

The young man answered without hesitation: "Feared."

"See?" Viper said. "You're smarter than I was at your age. What you did to Sticks Anderson this morning . . . impressive. By sundown, everybody in Harlem is gonna know about you. And folks will fear you before they even meet you."

"As long as you happy, Mr. Viper. That's all that matter to me."

"Keep in mind that Machiavelli said the best thing was to be loved *and* feared. Now that you've established your fearsomeness, I'd advise you to spread a little charm around when you meet folks."

Country flashed his gap-toothed grin. "Yessir, I can do that."

"That's what I figured."

*　*　*

Peewee's West was a sunbaked Southern Californian reflection of its East Coast main branch. While Lenox Avenue in Harlem had lost much of its prewar luster, so had Central Avenue in Los Angeles—where Peewee's West was located—found itself somewhat down at the heel by 1958. For decades, Central Avenue had mirrored central Harlem's heyday of thriving black enterprise and entertainment. The Dunbar Hotel, Elks Hall, the Club Alabam: homegrown L.A. talents as well as traveling jazz royalty from all over the country relished playing those venues. The Lincoln Theater proudly touted itself as the "West Coast Apollo." While "The Avenue," as Los Angelenos called it, had seen better days, Peewee's West was an instant hit when its doors opened. Some folks came for the music and the food. But word quickly spread that PW's was the indispensable address for scoring superb weed.

Late one evening, a broad-shouldered, dark-haired white man with droopy eyes approached Viper's booth in the corner of the club. At first, Viper wondered if he was a cop. Then, he had a feeling that would occur again and again during his visits to L.A. He thought he knew this person, the face was so familiar.

"Mind if I sit down?" the droopy-eyed man drawled.

That was when Viper realized that, yes, he knew that face, usually from seeing it blown up to superhuman proportions, in black-and-white, on the movie screen.

"Please have a seat, Mr. Mitchum."

"Call me 'Mitch,' reefer man."

It was the start of a beautiful connection. During his two-week stays in L.A. over the next year, Viper would become a regular at the poolside parties of Hollywood's most notorious potheads.

*   *   *

By the fall of 1959, Country Johnson had taken over so many responsibilities at Peewee's Harlem nightclub that Peewee himself started spending most of his time in Greenwich Village, where a relatively new market for their California Gold was exploding on the beatnik scene. Peewee had even become part owner of the Chiaroscuro coffeehouse on Bleecker Street. Viper dropped in one night, straight from the airport after one of his stints in L.A. The crowd was mixed. A bearded black poet took command of the microphone on the tiny stage. He recited in jagged bebop phrasing:

> *if you should see*
> *a man*
> *walking down a crowded street*
> *talking aloud*
> *to himself*
> *don't run*
> *in the opposite direction*
> *but run toward him*
> *for he is a POET!*
> *you have NOTHING to fear*
> *from the poet*
> *but the TRUTH*

The audience snapped their fingers instead of applauding. It was Ted Joans at the mike. He had been a good friend of Charlie Parker's; had taken Bird in after his wife, Chan, kicked him out; had even tried to get Bird off junk. Ted spotted the Viper in the house. Gave him a little salute.

Sally Anne Whitman Robinson, Peewee's high WASP bohemian wife, walked up to Viper and kissed him once on each cheek, European style. "Haven't seen you here in a while, good sir," she said a little archly. The Chiaroscuro's red brick walls were covered with artwork, mostly by Sally and her friends.

"Hey, Sally. What's up?"

"A bunch of new canvases, that's what's up. Interested in buying a painting?"

"Sure, Sally, I'll buy one of yours."

Sally took Viper by the hand and led him to a large, splotchy, colorful work hanging in the corner.

"You might like this one," she said. "I call it *Number Twenty-Three.*"

"Don't be tryin' to civilize this nigger, Sally," Peewee said, suddenly emerging from the backroom, where the weed was dealt.

"What's up, Peewee?" Viper said.

"Mom, Daddy said that word again!" A twelve-year-old girl with bronze skin and a mop of blond curls popped out from behind the bar/coffee counter. This was Wendy Robinson. Her eleven-year-old brother Peter Jr., who looked just like her, popped out right behind Wendy and chimed in his admonishment.

"You said you'd stop using that word, Dad!"

Even though it was a school night, Peewee and Sally's beautiful children were hanging out at the coffeehouse.

"They're right, Peewee," Sally said. "Try to set an example."

"All right, all right. Gimme a break. I'll wash my own mouth out with soap. But right now, leave me alone so I can talk to this nigger."

"Daaaaaaad!" Wendy and Peter Jr. squealed in unison.

"Step into my office, Viper," Peewee said. They entered the back room. Peewee closed the door behind them, fired up a joint, and passed it to the Viper. "How was L.A.?"

"Like you, Peewee, hipper all the time."

Peewee had changed his look over the years. He'd stopped straightening his hair, traded his fedora for a beret, his zoot suit for black turtlenecks, blue jeans, and leather jackets.

"Yeah, Viper," the little hipster said, "and you still lookin' like it's the 1940s. When you gonna get rid of that conk?"

"Somebody's got to keep Gentleman Jack in business. How are things up in Harlem?"

"Last I checked, everything was groovin'. In fact, Country's getting involved in the musical programming."

"So he's told me."

"You going to the club tomorrow night?"

"Of course."

"I'll be there, too."

*   *   *

"Wop bop a loo bop a lop bom bom!"

Little Richard, sporting a purple satin suit and a towering pompadour, shrieked from the stage of Peewee's nightclub. The packed house was delirious. Viper sat at a corner table with Peewee, Pork Chop, and Country Johnson, who had booked tonight's headliner.

"Rock 'n' roll is what's happenin', Mr. Viper," Country shouted over the noise. "Look at the crowd. The folks love it!"

"We're supposed to be a jazz club," Pork Chop said, barely audible over the roar of the public. Pork Chop was still the leader of the house band. But the crowds at the club had been shrinking. Folks kept coming around to buy reefer, of course, but they hadn't been staying for the music.

"We still a jazz club," Peewee said. "But Country's right. Let's program some rock 'n' roll once in a while."

Pork Chop had always been wary of Country, from that first meeting when the kid cut off Sticks Anderson's thumbs.

"You good with this, Clyde?"

Viper paused, then gave his honest opinion, knowing it would hurt his old friend to hear it.

"Can't argue with the cash register, Pork Chop. Like Country says: folks love it."

Pork Chop frowned, seemed almost to be biting his tongue.

"Thank you, Mr. Viper," Country said. "Thank you!"

Onstage, Little Richard twirled and shrieked:

"Wop bop a loo bop a lop bam boom!"

*   *   *

"Mmmmmmmmmm . . . MMM!" Randall "Country" Johnson hummed in pleasure as he tucked into his pig's feet, collard greens, and chitlins. "This sho is *deeeee-LICIOUS*, Mr. Viper. Thank you, sir!"

Viper smiled as he watched Country chow down. Viper himself was savoring his favorite dish on the menu: barbecued spare ribs and cornbread. He'd long ago asked Country to stop calling him "Mr." and "sir," but he realized by now that it was second nature to his courteous, Southern protégé. Country enjoyed showing Viper that bit of deference, and truth be told, Viper, at the age of forty-two, had come to like it.

In the fifteen months since he'd arrived in Harlem, Country had, in many ways, become citified. He wore sharp, bespoke suits (tailored by the ancient Seymour) and, like his boss, sported a Rolex on his wrist and drove two Cadillacs, though Country's were gold colored and midnight blue. But with his loping gait and gap-toothed grin, this ruthless young gangster could still exude a folksy charm. And he still talked like a hick.

Viper knew he was making a public statement by taking Country to dinner at the Red Rooster. It was midnight, and the restaurant was full and abuzz. Viper told Country he wanted to show his appreciation for his indispensable contribution to the enterprise this past year and a quarter. From making sure that none of their gage dealers dared to push junk to booking Little Richard and promoting change in the club's musical program, Country had succeeded beyond any reasonable expectation. Viper dining with him in as prominent a Harlem establishment as the famous Rooster signified a deadly dominance: two generations of reefer men to be revered and feared.

Count Basie and his entourage occupied a table nearby. The distinguished pianist and orchestra leader gave Viper a respectful nod when their eyes met. Viper returned the nod and thought, fleetingly, how surreal it was that someone he had worshipped much of his life would show him such a gesture of esteem. The royally monikered greats, Count Basie and Duke Ellington, held a special place in Viper's sphere. They were protean survivors in the long game, still swingin' with their big bands after three decades or more but adjusting with the times, welcoming bebop innovation, Basie had said, "so long as it made sense."

Basie usually played down on 52nd Street these days, but like so many of the jazzmen, he loved to eat and relax uptown, with his people. Viper noticed Basie's hands as he carved into his T-bone steak. They were fleshy on the backs and the palms but with exquisitely long fingers. Glancing at Count Basie's hands, then returning his gaze to Country Johnson wolfing down his soul food, Viper's mind flashed to Sticks Anderson.

Country Johnson had become instantly famous for chopping off Sticks Anderson's thumbs his first morning in Harlem. Pork Chop Bradley rushed Sticks to Harlem Hospital, where they staunched the bleeding and bandaged the wounds. Sticks left town on a Greyhound bus, headed south, that very day, never to be heard from again. Viper's taking Country to dinner at the Red Rooster let everyone know, in case anyone was in doubt, that the brutal young enforcer had Viper's full support.

"Glad you're enjoying the meal, Country," Viper said.

"Oh yeah," Country said, his mouth full. He dabbed at his greasy lips with the napkin he wore like a bib, tucked under his shirt collar. "Tastes like home."

Viper smiled. A sudden curiosity crossed his mind. "Do you ever get homesick, Country?"

The young gangster paused, seemed to consider the question seriously for the first time. "No, suh, can't say I do. I only been up in Harlem a year or so. Guess there be so much happenin' all the time, I ain't had time to miss bein' back home. But I wire money to my mama every week. So thank you for that, Mr. Viper."

"You're welcome, Country. But you're working damn hard to earn that money. And I appreciate it."

"How 'bout you, Mr. Viper?"

"Huh?"

"You ever get homesick?"

"Well, after more than twenty years, I guess Harlem *is* my home."

"Where you from, 'riginally?"

"Meachum, Alabama."

"We's a long way from down South up here, ain't we, Mr. Viper?"

"Yes, we are, Country."

At that moment, a buxom, brown-skinned beauty in a polka-dot dress sauntered by the table. Damn if she wasn't a dead ringer for Estella, who had given Viper "the first pussy he ever got in Harlem," way back in the day . . . before she became a hollow-eyed junkie and choked to death on her puke. The beauty batted her eyelashes at Country, and Viper shuddered when he heard her say to his protégé:

"Hey, killer."

Country flashed his gap-toothed grin. "Hey, baby. Wait for me by the bar. I see you after we finish dinner."

After she wiggled off to the bar, Viper leered and said, "You're a popular young man."

"Yeah, Mr. Viper," Country said with a wink. "Work hard, play hard. That's what they say, ain't it?"

"That was my motto when I was your age, Country."

"Proud to follow in your footsteps, sir."

They ate in comfortable silence for a while. Then, Country said:

"Can I ask you a kinda personal question, Mr. Viper?"

"Depends on the question."

"How come you ain't married?"

Viper chuckled. "Never met the right woman, I guess."

"Really? Nobody?"

"Well, there was this one girl. Years ago. But she left Harlem. She lives far away now."

"Really? And you ain't never found nobody else?"

"I figure I never wanted to."

Country paused and chewed reflectively. Swallowed slowly. "Is you heartbroken, Mr. Viper?"

The question startled Viper. No one, not even Pork Chop, had ever asked him that. He paused, then answered, he thought, truthfully:

"No."

9

THE LONG HIGH. THAT WAS how the Viper would come to think of the five months in the middle of 1960: a period of dreamy elevation, when, whether he had smoked any herb or not, he lived in a heightened state that could suddenly leave him staggered, often feeling both alert and spaced out, sharp and numb, acutely attuned to certain things happening in the moment and oblivious to other, much more important, matters. The Long High felt like a sublime, exalted state, a new level of consciousness and being. The Long High was, ultimately, like any other high: it couldn't possibly last.

It began in April 1960. Dan Miller, self-satisfied senior partner at Schneider, Miller, and Bloom, invited Viper Morton to his law office for another after-hours meeting. Once again, he broke out the whiskey and cigars.

"Viper, I can't commend you enough for the outstanding job you've done. Our marijuana operations have expanded greatly in the past two years. The farm in the Sonoma Valley is growing to industrial size. At any given time, we've got a couple hundred Mexican migrant workers tending to the crop. And still, demand is outstripping supply. So we're planning to diversify. There's a lawyer in Paris named Pierre Marchand. He says he can establish a supply chain from Indochina. I'd like to send you to Paris to meet Marchand, sample the product, and discuss the possibilities."

"Paris?" Viper said. "When?"

"I've booked you on a flight two days from now," Dan Miller said. "Stay a couple of weeks. We'll call it a working vacation. You've earned it."

Paris. From the moment Viper left Miller's office until the time he boarded the plane forty-eight hours later, he felt spellbound. This was the start of the Long High. He knew that going to Paris would mean seeing Yolanda. It was inevitable. His mind swirled with memories he had suppressed for twelve years.

Yolanda, chic in her beige cashmere coat, snuggling into his shoulder on the bench in Riverside Park.

Yo-Yo in her plaid bathrobe, making him and Pretty Paul a breakfast of steak and eggs and grits.

Yo-Yo in the park again, her left eye blue, bruised, swollen shut.

The feel of Yo-Yo in his arms, the arousing scent of her, in the room above Lady Athena's beauty parlor, holding her close after he'd told her her husband was dead.

Yolanda in dark sunglasses and a black dress, the mourning widow, belting out her grief in Saint Peter's church.

Yo-Yo in his apartment, telling him she was leaving for Paris.

All these memories he had locked in a mental drawer. The drawer had now exploded open and transformed into a kaleidoscopic vision of Yolanda DeVray: enchanting the audience at the Apollo, beaming in the baptism of their applause; writhing naked in Viper's bed; grunting like a feral cat, crouched in the corner of Mr. O's bedroom, her maid's uniform streaked with blood, dagger-like weapon in her hand.

If he had thought of Yolanda at all over the past dozen years, she had seemed like a figment of his imagination. Now, at the start of the Long High, when he knew he would see her again in Paris, the memories became as vivid as hallucinations.

*   *   *

Viper landed in Paris on a Friday afternoon. A uniformed chauffeur greeted him at the airport and drove him to his suite at the Ritz Hotel, where he had half an hour to freshen up, then took him to his rendezvous at the law office of Pierre Marchand on the Champs Élysées.

"Welcome, Monsieur Clyde Morton," the thin, silver-haired attorney said. "What a pleasure it is to meet you at last."

"Good afternoon, Mr. Marchand."

"Is this your first time in Paris?"

"It's my first time in Europe."

They engaged in small talk for a while, then a gorgeous secretary came in with a silver platter. On it was an elegant wooden pipe, a gold lighter, and a little ceramic bowl full of grass.

"This is known as Thai stick," Marchand said, "originating from Thailand, naturally. Please, have a taste."

Viper ignited, inhaled, exhaled, savored the taste on his tongue, waited for the high to kick in. Ah, yes . . .

From this moment on, the Long High he already felt would be enhanced by the high of Thai stick.

"We represent an exporter of tea from Asia," Marchand said, taking a hit on the pipe. "It would provide us with an excellent means of transporting marijuana to the United States."

"I like the product, Mr. Marchand."

"Please, call me Pierre."

"Call me Viper."

"Shall we take a tour of Paris?"

The chauffeur drove Pierre Marchand and Viper all over town. Clyde Morton—born in Spooner, Georgia, raised in Meachum, Alabama—was awestruck. Viper felt like he had when he'd been nineteen years old and Peewee and Mr. O had shown him New York from the back of a Rolls-Royce. He tried not to gawp as Marchand's driver guided the sleek Citroën DS down tree-lined boulevards, past gushing fountains. Viper felt like he was in a movie as he gazed upon sights he had only seen before in the movies: the Eiffel Tower, the Arc de Triomphe, Notre-Dame Cathedral. Marchand and Viper smoked more Thai marijuana in the back of the car. The intensity of the Long High escalated, coolly but inexorably, smoothly but exhilaratingly.

"I propose that we have a traditional French dinner," Marchand said, "at one of my favorite restaurants. Escargots, confit de canard, fine wines, and fragrant cheeses. What do you say, Viper?"

"I say, 'Oui, oui, Pierre.'"

"And after, we go to a jazz club. In Saint-Germain. Chez Rémy. I believe you know the owner, Rémy Arnaud."

Here it was. The moment Viper knew would come.

"Yes, I know him."

"I will leave the car and chauffeur at your disposal," Pierre Marchand said. "By the way, a singer who is performing tonight, she talks about you quite a lot. Do you remember her, from New York? Yolanda DeVray?"

"Yes, Pierre, I remember her."

*   *   *

Viper and Marchand arrived at the jazz club at midnight. No sooner had they sat down than Yolanda DeVray took the stage. Yo-Yo stared straight at Viper, a long, soulful look. Then she opened her mouth to sing.

Yo-Yo was thirty-nine-years-old. She was no longer a pretty young thing. But she was more beautiful than ever, radiant in a slinky black gown. She truly was a star now, a woman in full. She stared straight at Viper as she sang, her voice still fierce and angelic, suffused with pain but now with another quality—a wisdom, a dark knowledge, an embrace of life in all its blissful, tragic mystery. Yo-Yo finished her set, and as the crowd exploded in applause, she seemed to glide from the stage to the empty chair at Viper's table. Pierre Marchand, the waiters and customers, the emcee and the other acts, everyone else seemed to disappear.

This is where the Long High really kicked in. The combination of suppressed memories rushing back, the cinematic splendor of Paris, the power of the Thai dope, the sight, the sound of Yolanda again, his beautiful, dangerous Yo-Yo, here before him, in the luscious flesh: Viper felt overwhelmed, as if he were about to burst into laughter, or burst into tears.

"Clyde, I've waited so long for you to come to Paris," Yo-Yo said. "Did you ever get my letters?"

"I threw them all away without opening them," Viper answered truthfully.

"That's what I was afraid of." She took his hand in hers. "I was such a fool, Clyde. Can you forgive me?"

"I want to."

"Take me away from here, Clyde. Right now."

Pierre Marchand stayed at Chez Rémy, and the chauffeur drove Viper and Yo-Yo to the suite at the Ritz. They made love to each other for only the second time. It was as tender and passionate, as sublime and ecstatic as Viper had remembered. He fell into a deep sleep, his body entwined with Yolanda's.

*   *   *

"Clyde, wake up, Clyde."

Viper opened his eyes, wondering if he had dreamt the previous evening. But no. There was Yolanda, sitting on the edge of the bed, in a white Ritz Hotel bathrobe. Sunlight was streaming through the gauzy curtains.

The Long High was still just beginning.

"I ordered us coffee and croissants from room service," she said. "Get up, baby. I want to show you this beautiful city."

Over the next two weeks, Viper held daily business meetings with Pierre Marchand, planning their new enterprise for shipping Asian marijuana to the USA. But Viper spent most of his time with Yo-Yo. She introduced him to her many Parisian friends and admirers, at the Café de Flore, les Deux Magots, La Coupole.

Yo-Yo and Viper were rediscovering each other. Or, perhaps, truly discovering each other . . . for the very first time . . .

"You were the only person who ever really cared about me, Clyde," she told him one afternoon as they cuddled on a bench in the garden of the Palais Royal. "You were the only one. I'm just so sorry I was too young and foolish to understand."

Yolanda showed Viper the Jardin du Luxembourg and the Tuileries. She took him to the Louvre and more museums than he could remember the names of, and started to teach him about art.

"I have a pet theory," she said, "about certain painters and jazz musicians. Do you want to hear it?"

"Of course, Yo-Yo."

"Louis Armstrong and Duke Ellington are like Renoir and Monet. Count Basie is Degas. Charlie Parker is Van Gogh, of course. Dizzy Gillespie is Gauguin. Thelonious Monk is Cézanne. Miles Davis is Picasso, and John Coltrane is Matisse. Do you see what I mean?"

"Not really, Yo-Yo." Viper laughed, touched by how seriously she expressed her theory. "You'll have to keep educating me."

Most nights, Viper watched Yo-Yo perform at Chez Rémy. They would have a late dinner, then return to the Ritz to make sweet love.

At this point, Viper felt a satisfying sense of reconciliation, of culmination. Yo-Yo had made up for all the hurt she had caused him. This romantic Paris interlude had healed all the old wounds. All was forgiven. He would go back to New York. She would stay in Paris. And, maybe—as Yo-Yo had infuriated him by suggesting twelve years ago—he would visit her from time to time. While in town, on business . . .

But no. The Long High was destined to continue . . .

"Clyde," Yolanda said one night, as they lay in each other's arms in their bed at the Ritz. "I want to go back to New York. With you. To stay."

"But why? You've made such a wonderful life for yourself here in Paris."

"I'm homesick, Clyde. I miss Harlem. I miss our people. I miss fried chicken and cornbread. And I miss you, Clyde. I want to be with you."

"Listen, Yo-Yo. I shut you out of my mind for twelve years. These past two weeks have been beautiful. But my life in America . . . is different. And the history between us . . . well . . ."

"You don't know if you can trust me. I understand, Clyde. But I'll show you. I'm ready. I'm ready to come home. And I'm ready for you."

*　　*　　*

The Long High grew ever more intense when Viper and Yolanda arrived in New York together in May 1960. Despite the euphoria Viper felt, he remained lucid about certain details, as one will, even when high. He returned to his luxurious apartment in the art deco building on Edgecombe Avenue on Sugar Hill. But he installed Yolanda in his old flat in the brownstone he now owned on Lenox Avenue. He wasn't ready for them to live together.

"I understand, Clyde," Yolanda said. "You want to take it slow. But we have time. We have the rest of our lives."

A day after his return, Viper called a meeting with Peewee, Pork Chop, and Country at the nightclub.

"Say what?" Peewee shrieked. "Yolanda's back in Harlem?"

"Yes," Viper said, "and I'm going to be managing her career. I'd like her to sing with Pork Chop and the band here."

Pork Chop was thrilled. "Great, Viper! That'll help bring the jazz crowds back."

"Hope that works with your rock 'n' roll programming, Country."

"It all sound mighty fine to me, Mr. Viper," Country said, flashing his gap-toothed grin.

"My idea is to introduce her gradually to the public," Viper said. "Four months performing here. Then, in the fall, get her some gigs down on 52nd Street. And by the end of the year, we can cut her first album."

"You got it all figured out, huh, Viper?" Peewee said. "But how you gonna be a manager, deal with the new product comin' from overseas, and handle the business in New York and at Peewee's West?"

"I think Country's ready to take on more responsibilities in New York," Viper said. "Aren't you, Country?"

"Yessir, Mr. Viper. I sho am!"

"So, Viper," Peewee said, "you fuckin' her or what?"

"Peewee!" Pork Chop shouted.

Viper and Peewee stared hard into each other's eyes. "If I am," Viper said evenly, "would that be a problem?"

"Not for *me*, man. But it might turn out to be a problem for *you*."

*   *   *

The past had come crashing into the present. Under the influence of the Long High, it all seemed to make sense to Viper. There seemed to be a cosmic logic, an inevitability to it all as he watched Peewee take the stage at the club that had once belonged to Mr. O but now belonged to his chauffeur, to introduce Mr. O's former maid and sex slave, Yo-Yo, at her first performance as a jazz singer since returning from Paris a week earlier. It was standing room only. Yolanda's reputation had preceded her.

"Well, I ain't seen this many folks in the club since Little Richard played here," the emcee said in his high-pitched voice. "Even the Baroness de Koenigswarter is in the house! How ya doin', Nica? Now, a lot of y'all might be too young to remember tonight's headliner. I remember her, though. I remember a whole lotta shit she might like to forget. But whatever. Here she is, direct from Paris, the famous femme fatale of Harlem in the Forties: Yolanda DeVray!"

Yolanda seemed a little skittish as she took the microphone from Peewee. "Good evening, everybody. Thank you so much for coming out tonight. Lord, I'm feeling so many emotions. I've been away for twelve years. And . . . well, since I can't say all that's in my heart, let me just sing for you."

The moment Yo-Yo opened her mouth to sing, the crowd was enraptured. She gave a magnificent performance. And when she came off stage, she threw her arms around the Viper. That's when everybody knew that finally, at long last, after all these years, Yo-Yo belonged to him, and him alone.

"Thank you, Clyde," Yolanda whispered in his ear as they held each other tight. "Thank you for this second chance."

*   *   *

Harlem seemed brighter during the Long High. Yolanda DeVray seemed to bring back a touch of glamor to Lenox Avenue. She rekindled her friendship with Lady Athena, regaling the gals at the beauty parlor with tales of her adventuresome years in Paris.

The jazz crowds swarmed back to Peewee's. But Peewee himself made sure to stay down in Greenwich Village on nights when Yolanda performed in the club that bore his name.

Over the next three months, Viper and Yolanda fell into a sort of pleasant routine. He had his apartment on Sugar Hill. She had hers on Lenox Avenue. He spent two weeks a month in L.A. And whenever they were together, every moment felt charged with energy, an emotional and erotic intensity that came to define the Long High.

One afternoon, Viper was walking out of Gentleman Jack's barbershop, hair freshly straightened, as Country Johnson was heading into the shop for a fresh conk of his own.

"So, Mr. Viper," Country said, grinning knowingly. "Miss Yolanda. She was the one, right? The one that got away."

Viper felt strangely touched by Country's insight. And by the fact that his young protégé actually seemed happy for him.

"Yeah, Country," Viper said. "She's the one."

"Congrats," Country said with a wink. "She a trophy if ever there was one."

"Thank you, Country," Viper said, smiling shyly.

The Long High. Maybe it was what other people called being in love.

One evening in late August, Viper entered the apartment on Lenox Avenue and saw Yolanda standing at the table with a bottle of red wine and a wooden platter filled with cheese and sausage.

"Look, Clyde, I found a wonderful shop downtown. All French products!"

Viper noticed an oddly shaped knife. The blade was very sharp and tapered, the handle made of horn. "What the hell is that?"

"It's a Laguiole knife," Yolanda said. "Specially made in the Occitan region of France. Isn't it beautiful?"

"Indeed it is. Are we celebrating something?"

"Don't be coy, Clyde. The Club Downbeat called me today. You booked me for an entire week in October?"

"You've earned it."

"Oh, Clyde. Thank you for this new life!"

They drank the French wine, ate the French cheese and sausage, and made sweet love all night. It felt like the Long High would go on forever.

*   *   *

The next day, Viper left for another two-week stint in L.A. Over the last five days of his stay, Yo-Yo didn't phone. That was unusual. The few times Viper called her, there was no answer. Also unusual. He told himself there was nothing to worry about. But by the time Viper landed back in New York, he was starting to panic.

It was midnight when he entered the apartment, Yolanda's apartment, on Lenox Avenue. The living room was dark, but the bedroom light was on.

Viper nearly screamed when he saw Yo-Yo laid out on the bed, eyes closed, wearing only her bra and panties.

He saw the kit on the night stand. The syringe, the burnt spoon, the rubber tube, the lighter, and the empty wax paper.

He saw track marks on her left arm. He smelled urine. She'd wet herself.

He put his arms around her, relieved to find her body was still warm. She was breathing.

He wrapped her in a blanket and carried her downstairs, out to the street.

People stared as the Viper rushed with his bundle to his black Cadillac, parked right outside the brownstone. The onlookers gaped as he revved the engine and pulled away.

Viper raced into the emergency room of Harlem Hospital, carrying Yo-Yo in his arms. Medics whisked her away, behind closed doors. Viper spent the next three hours pacing in the waiting room. Finally, a doctor emerged.

"Mr. Morton," he said, "she's still unconscious, but her condition has stabilized. She's going to be all right."

Viper slumped in a chair, relieved, exhausted, disoriented. How was this possible? How did this happen?

Around four in the morning, Country Johnson appeared.

"How ya doin', Mr. Viper? I heard what happened. She gonna be okay?"

"Yes," Viper said, "the doctors say she'll be all right. But . . . I don't understand. Yo-Yo didn't shoot up."

Country paused and stared at the floor a long time before speaking again.

"Mr. Viper, I think this just started in the past week or so. I seen Miss Yolanda after hours at the club, talkin' with Mr. Peewee."

"Peewee?"

Country continued, haltingly, trying to choose his words with care. "I've had my suspicions, Mr. Viper. All summer long. I didn't wanna say nothin' 'cause I wasn't sure. But I think Mr. Peewee been dealin' heroin. And I think he the one musta sold that junk to Miss Yolanda."

Viper absorbed what Country told him, walked to a phone booth in the hospital lobby, and called the club. Peewee answered. They agreed to meet on the rooftop at five o'clock, just the two of them.

* * *

Viper and Peewee confronted each other in the open air, high above the streets of Harlem. Pigeons warbled. A seagull screeched overhead. Delivery trucks rolled by along the avenue, six flights below.

"Don't lie to me, Peewee!"

"I ain't lyin', Viper. I've been selling junk. A little bit here and there. But I never sold shit to Yolanda."

"Why should I believe that you sold junk, but not to her?"

"You just blinded by that crazy bitch! Why you think she jumped on you in Paris? Her career wasn't goin' nowhere over there. She's just usin' you to get her a recording contract, make her name over here."

"You've never forgiven her for dumping your ass twenty years ago."

"Open your damn eyes, Viper. The bitch is nothin' but trouble."

"Stop calling her that."

"I ain't got time for this shit."

Then, Peewee made his fatal mistake. He turned his back to his friend, headed for the staircase. Viper, furious, grabbed him from behind.

"Lemme go, you crazy motherfucker!" Peewee screamed.

They scuffled and struggled, twirled about, moving closer to the edge of the rooftop. Peewee reached into his leather jacket, pulled out his pistol. Viper grabbed his wrist, twisted it. Peewee dropped the gun. Viper and Peewee were thrashing violently. They were at the ledge when Viper finally took control of the struggle. He grasped Peewee by his right arm and right leg. His left arm and left leg were flailing and kicking in the air, over the edge of the rooftop.

"I'm tellin' you, Viper," Peewee screamed, "I didn't give Yo-Yo the junk!"

"But you admit you're dealin' it!"

"Fuck yeah! It's fucking supply and demand, nigger! What the fuck is wrong with you?"

That's when Viper let Peewee go.

The sound of his body splattering on the sidewalk was unlike anything Viper had heard since the war, the Pacific Theater, a cross between a splash and an explosion.

Viper picked up Peewee's pistol from the rooftop, tucked it in his pocket. He hurried downstairs and out the back door of the empty nightclub. Called his friend the cop from a phone booth.

"Hello?"

"Good morning, Detective Carney."

"Viper, is that you?"

"I'd like to report a suicide. Somebody jumped off the rooftop of Peewee's."

Viper hung up and walked briskly back to his home on Sugar Hill.

The Long High was over.

10

TELL ME, VIPER, WHAT ARE your three wishes?

It was a quarter to two in the middle of the night of Viper Morton's third murder, in November 1961, fourteen months after his second killing, a crime he did not regret: dropping Peewee off the rooftop of his nightclub. Fifteen minutes from now, Detective Red Carney, if true to the threat he had made, would show up in Weehawken, New Jersey, where Viper sat on a couch in the vast living room of the Cathouse, surrounded by twenty jazz musicians and more than a hundred felines, stoned on Thai stick, staggered by grief, contemplating the question his hostess, the Baroness Pannonica de Koenigswarter, had asked him. Looking back on his life, a life he knew might end this night, he'd scribbled down two wishes. He had just one wish left.

Pork Chop Bradley sat on the other side of the room, softly plucking his bass. Pork Chop had watched Viper closely since he'd returned from Nica's bedroom, where he'd taken Carney's threatening phone call. Viper saw an infinite sorrow in his old friend's eyes. Pork Chop had known the truth. It was obvious. Maybe everyone had known. Everyone except the Viper.

That was when it came to him. Viper lifted the notepad and pencil from the coffee table and wrote down his third wish.

*　*　*

I am speaking now of September 1960. Dawn was breaking. An hour after tossing Peewee to his death and picking up the gun the little gangster had dropped, Viper was back in his apartment on Sugar Hill. He opened his bedroom closet, looking for a place to stash Peewee's pistol. All his years in this dangerous business, Viper had never carried a gun. In the back of the closet, he came across the hard case. He hadn't seen it in years. He opened it and stared at the trumpet his father had brought back from France. The trumpet that had led young Clyde Morton to catch a train to New York. That had led him to Pork Chop, Estella, Mr. O, Peewee, West Indian Charlie, Big Al, Pretty Paul and Buttercup and Yolanda DeVray. And when Viper went to France himself, he didn't come back with a trumpet. He came back with Yo-Yo. Peewee was right. That bitch was nothing but trouble. Viper stashed Peewee's gun in the case with the horn, shoved it in the back of the closet. Then he collapsed, fully clothed, on the bed. He hadn't slept all night. He'd been too busy pacing the hospital waiting room, hoping Yo-Yo would survive her heroin overdose. He fell into a deep sleep.

Viper nearly leapt off the bed at the shock of the rattling phone. He glanced at the clock. It was ten in the morning.

"Hello?"

"Viper, it's Dan Miller. I've been on the phone with Red Carney. He told me what happened to Yolanda. And to Peewee. I just want you to know that whatever the reason Peewee decided to kill himself, it won't affect our business relationship."

"Thank you, Dan. Peewee was dealing junk. I figure he got in trouble with the Mafia and decided to end his own life before some Guido did it for him."

"Yes, that sounds plausible. Our firm has moved to take ownership of the Harlem club. And it will still be called Peewee's."

"Glad to hear it."

"Another thing," Miller said, his tone softening. "This is more personal. Clearly, Yolanda has a heroin problem. I'd like to transfer her to a clinic in Connecticut, where she can be treated. The firm will pay for all the expenses. We'll have a private ambulance service take her there this morning."

"Thank you, Dan," Viper said, genuinely touched. "Thank you so much."

"You're family, Viper."

No sooner had he hung up with Dan Miller than Detective Red Carney called.

"Viper, get your black ass in my office right now!"

Carney had grown bloated and even ruddier over the years. On this morning, the rogue cop was nearly purple with rage as he paced back and forth across the floor of the same small, nondescript office he'd occupied for more than two decades. The Viper sat in front of him, coolly smoking a cigarette.

"Another suicide, huh, Viper?"

"So it seems."

"Peewee was one of your oldest friends. He landed head first, you know. They had to scrape his brains off the sidewalk, then hose down the pavement."

"That's a damn shame."

"Left behind a wife and two kids."

"Yeah, well, maybe Sally's family will take her back now."

"Viper, I don't know what the fuck is going on with you, but this puts all of us at risk."

"How so?"

"Don't you read the damn papers? The FBI is gonna be cracking down on illegal drug traffic like never before. Easy targets, good PR. Hoover is desperate to hold on to his job, no matter who the next president is. The feds have always left our operation alone, but you've got a reputation, Viper. If your colleagues start dying, J. Edgar might decide to make an example out of you. Our whole enterprise could be threatened."

"What's your point, Red?"

"My point is, next time somebody in our circle turns up dead, I'm coming after you, Viper. We've had a good thing going on here for many years. But I'll sacrifice you to save the enterprise."

"That's what I figured."

*   *   *

Late that afternoon, the Viper drove up to Connecticut. The countryside was stunning, the leaves just starting to change color. The private clinic was clearly a bastion of the rich and white. When he pulled into the driveway in his silver Cadillac, the doctors, nurses, and patients walking the grounds stared at Viper, stupefied. The nurse at the front desk flashed a rigid smile.

"Miss DeVray is waiting for you on the veranda," she said.

Yolanda sat in a deck chair on the stone patio, dressed in a hospital gown and wrapped in a blanket. She looked exhausted.

"Hello, Clyde."

Viper sat in a rattan chair beside her. "How are you feeling, Yo-Yo?"

"Physically, I'm fine. But, my God, Clyde, I feel so sick in my soul. I am so sorry. Can you ever forgive me?"

"There's nothing to forgive."

"That's not true. I never told you that I shot up for the first time years ago, with Paul. I tried it again in Paris. I liked it. But it was never a habit. The last week or so, I did it again. And I . . . oh, Clyde . . ."

"Don't say any more, Yo-Yo. You don't have to explain anything."

"I heard about Peewee. Another suicide . . .?"

"Yes."

"This is all so hard to understand."

"You don't need to understand. You just need to get better. Dan Miller says they'll keep you here for a month of treatment."

"Yes. They call it rehabilitation. What I want to know, Clyde, is will you be there for me when I get out?"

Viper didn't answer. He just held her hand as they stared at the sunset.

Yolanda would only make it through two weeks of her rehabilitation. Her mother fell sick, and Yo-Yo decided to go back to New Orleans to be with her. Viper drove her to the airport.

"They think it's a cancer," Yolanda told him in the car. "This could be a long, slow end."

"I'm sorry, Yo-Yo."

"I'm being punished for my sins. That's what's happening."

"Don't think that way."

"I just want you to know that I'll be back. Don't give up on me, Clyde. Please don't give up on me."

Through the glass wall of the terminal, Viper watched Yo-Yo as she walked across the tarmac and up the stairs to board the plane. She turned and blew him a kiss, tears in her eyes. He waved goodbye and tried not to show how shattered he felt. Driving back to Harlem, Viper vowed to do what he had done before, for twelve long years: to shut Yolanda completely out of his mind.

*   *   *

Viper was used to inspiring fear in Harlem, but after Pee-wee's death, folks seemed scared even to look him in the eye. Not Country Johnson, though.

"Don't you worry 'bout nothin', Mr. Viper," his trusted lieutenant told him a week after Peewee's fall. "The club is doin' better than ever. Big crowds, lotsa money. The reefer business is explodin' and ain't nobody in our crew gonna even *think* about dealin' junk *now*."

Viper felt oddly comforted by Country's words. "I want to thank you," he said, "for coming by the hospital that night and telling me what you told me."

"You can rely on me, Mr. Viper. Always."

That same week, Pork Chop quit his job as bandleader at the club.

"That's right, Clyde," he said. "Call it early retirement. I'm gonna be one of those old men in the barbershop, talkin' shit and playin' checkers all day."

They didn't talk about what had happened to Yolanda or Peewee. Viper didn't know if Pork Chop had known that Peewee was dealing junk or that Yo-Yo was shooting up. He wanted to believe he hadn't known. But certainly Pork Chop knew that Peewee hadn't committed suicide. He must have known that Viper had done what he had to do. But he wanted to keep his distance for now.

"Oh, I'll still come by the club once in a while," Pork Chop said with forced joviality. "But I figure Country will program even more rock 'n' roll now, and I'm too old for that shit."

"I understand, Pork Chop. Take good care of yourself."

"You, too, Clyde."

*　*　*

A year passed. Viper continued to travel frequently to L.A. And he made another trip to Paris, a brief one, to discuss business with Pierre Marchand. He thrived, bitterly.

Yolanda was not on his mind, not even in his dreams. But there she stood, as he stepped out of his building on Sugar Hill late one morning in the summer of '61, waiting for him on the sidewalk.

"Hello, Clyde."

She looked absolutely radiant, her honey-gold skin shining, her emerald eyes sparkling. What was the strange power this woman held over him?

"Aren't you happy to see me?"

"Sure, Yo-Yo."

Viper tried to play the tough guy, but he could feel his heart melting, his bitterness evaporating.

"Did you get any of my letters this past year?"

"What do you think?"

"You threw them away without reading them."

Viper nodded.

"Let's talk, Clyde. Why don't you invite me up to your apartment?"

They spent the whole day making love. Yolanda owned him, body and soul. She had since the first time he'd ever laid eyes on her, in Mr. O's den, twenty-three years ago.

"I'm back here to stay, Clyde," Yolanda said as they lay in bed naked, their bodies entwined.

"Your mother?" Viper asked hesitantly.

"She died in July. Two weeks later, my father had a heart attack and died."

"I'm so sorry."

"They were so much in love. One of them couldn't go on living without the other. They knew what was important in life. I think I finally know, too."

"What do you want to do now?"

"I want to pick up where we left off, before I started shooting up again. I begged you last year, Clyde. Please don't give up on me."

Things happened quickly from there. Viper still wasn't ready to have Yo-Yo move in, so he installed her again in his old apartment on Lenox Avenue. It took some tense negotiating, and a bit of bribery, but he got the Downbeat on 52nd Street to give Yo-Yo that weeklong engagement they'd had to cancel last year. And finally, in November,

Yo-Yo cut her first album. Pork Chop came out of retirement to lead her band. Viper was there at the studio for the two days of recording. Yo-Yo had never sung more gorgeously.

"So what are we gonna call this album?" Pork Chop asked after they finished the final number.

"I don't know," the songstress said. "I guess we should ask my manager."

"How about *Yolanda DeVray*," Viper said, "*A New Beginning*?"

"I like it," Pork Chop said. "I like it a lot."

"Thank you, Clyde," Yo-Yo said. "Thank you for not giving up on me."

* * *

It was true. The Viper had not given up on Yolanda. But he still did not entirely trust her. The day after she finished the album, he left for L.A. It was his first trip out West since Yo-Yo had returned to Harlem. He was supposed to stay for two weeks. But without alerting Yo-Yo, he came back five days early.

He entered the apartment on Lenox Avenue silently. Ten o'clock at night. The living room was deserted, the lights turned low. He saw on the table an empty bottle of wine and two half-full glasses, a wooden platter with a few slices of sausage and cheese, and the Laguiole knife, with its sharp, tapered blade and polished horn handle. The light was on in the bedroom. He heard a man's voice. He picked up the knife and walked slowly toward the bedroom door.

"Come on, baby," the man said. "Wake up. Gimme some lovin'."

Viper pushed open the bedroom door. He saw the syringe on the nightstand. He saw Yo-Yo stretched out on the bed, wearing only her bra and panties. And he saw Country Johnson, wearing only a pair of boxer shorts, writhing on top of her.

"Come on, baby," Country said, "wake up."

"You motherfucker!" Viper exploded.

Country twisted around, terror in his eyes. "Mr. Viper! What the fuck you doin' back?"

Country leapt from the bed. Viper approached him slowly, gripping the knife.

"It ain't what you think, Mr. Viper," Country pleaded. "Hold on now." He held up his hands, continued to back away from Viper, across the bedroom floor. "Wait now, just hold on."

Viper grabbed Country by the throat, pushed him against the wall. Country was about to fight back, when Viper plunged the knife into his belly.

"Aaaccchhh!"

Viper twisted the knife.

"Daddy!" Country said. "Daddy!"

Staring into Country's eyes, Viper saw it for the first time. Country gazed at him, wide-eyed, in agony. And suddenly Viper knew. He knew this was his son.

"Daddy!" Country gasped.

Viper was still in a rage. He dragged the knife upward, toward Country's heart, slicing open his body. He pulled out the knife and backed away. Country slid down the wall, blood pouring out of him. Viper had to step away to avoid it spilling on his shoes.

"Daddy . . ." Country groaned.

Then he fell silent. Viper walked over to Yo-Yo, sprawled on the bed, the syringe and the packet of heroin at her side. She was groggy.

"Clyde, is that you?"

He grabbed her by the hair, held the knife to her slender throat.

"Do it," Yolanda murmured. "Do it, Clyde. Kill me."

The bloody Laguiole knife was almost touching her flesh. Viper's hand quavered.

"Do it," Yolanda said. "I deserve it."

Viper let go of her. He threw the knife to the floor and bolted out of the apartment.

He drove to his home on Sugar Hill, took a shower, changed into a fresh suit. He opened the bedroom closet, grabbed Peewee's gun from the trumpet case, and tucked it in his jacket pocket. Then, for reasons he didn't understand, Viper went back out to Lenox Avenue. He called Red Carney from a phone booth. After all that had happened, he was still trying to save Yo-Yo.

"Get a patrol car over to Yolanda's apartment. And an ambulance."

"Is there somebody dead?" Carney asked.

"Yeah."

"I can give you three hours. No more."

* * *

Nearly three hours later, Viper rose from the couch at the Cathouse and, clutching the notepad with his three wishes scribbled on it, walked over to Pork Chop, sat down beside him. Pork Chop stopped plucking his bass.

"Time's up, Clyde?"

"Just about. I'm supposed to meet Red Carney outside."

"So you're gonna surrender?"

"Well, I've got a gun on me. I might shoot it out."

"Jesus, Clyde."

"So, tell me, Pork Chop. You knew. You knew who Country was."

"Yes."

"How?"

"About a year after Country showed up in New York," Pork Chop said, "I was ridin' a train down to Arkansas, on my way to the funeral of my best friend from boyhood. I was sitting alone in the dining car when a Pullman porter came up to me. He was in bad shape. Frail. Sickly. He kept coughing. Said he was dying of emphysema."

"Thaddeus," Viper whispered.

"Your brother recognized me. Seemed to know a whole lot about your life . . . in New York *and* Los Angeles."

"*The Pullman Porters are a nationwide network, Mr. Bradley,*" *Thaddeus had said.* "*We know many things.*"

"He told me about the girl you'd left behind," Pork Chop told Viper at the Cathouse. "Bertha slit her throat when she was nine months pregnant but the baby survived."

"*Little Randall was sent to live with Bertha's sister and her husband in Mississippi,*" *Thaddeus told Pork Chop on the train, two years earlier.*

"*But Country Johnson don't look nothin' like Clyde Morton,*" *Pork Chop said to Thaddeus.*

"*No,*" *Thaddeus said,* "*he takes after his mother's side of the family.*"

"*Country said his daddy died from a morphine addiction.*"

"That was his step-daddy. I followed Randall's life from afar. He didn't know who his real father was . . . until I told him."

"You met with him?" Pork Chop asked.

Thaddeus started slapping his palm down on the table in the dining car. He lifted his head, raised his eyes heavenward. "It was God's doing! It had to be the Lord's intervention."

"What happened? When?"

"Randall was ridin' the train from Kansas City to New York last year," Thaddeus said, his voice now taking on the intonation of a preacher in the pulpit. "I knew who he was. I knew he'd gotten mixed up in gangsterdom. The fact that I met him when I did . . . it had to be God's doing."

"Does Clyde know?"

"Only if Randall told him. But they're both doomed. God showed me in a vision. I'll be dead soon. I hope to see Randall again in the kingdom of Heaven. But my brother, he's goin' straight to Hell."

"Why didn't you tell me, Pork Chop?" Viper said at the Cathouse.

"I didn't think it was my place," Pork Chop said. "And I thought maybe you knew. I thought maybe that was why you were so fond of Country."

"Did Yolanda know?"

"I have no idea. But I knew Country was gettin' close to her. What I didn't know was that he was dealin' junk."

Viper let out a long, deep breath. He struggled to absorb all this.

"What did Country want?" he asked, feeling tears sting his eyes again. "Why didn't he tell me the truth?"

"I think it was a love–hate thing, Clyde. He loved you and wanted you to recognize him, and at the same time, he hated you and wanted to do you harm. He might have blamed you for his mother's death. So he wanted to hurt you by harming the woman you loved."

A car horn honked.

"That'll be Red," the Viper said.

"Be careful, Clyde."

"Goodbye, Pork Chop."

He rose and walked over to the baroness.

"So, Viper, have you finished your list?"

"Here it is, Nica."

The baroness took the notepad in a slightly trembling hand, raised the eyeglasses that hung from a chain around her neck, and peering through them, read the list silently to herself, her lips moving almost imperceptibly:

One: I wish I'd never left home.
Two: I wish she had loved me.
Three: I wish someone had told me the truth.

Nica lowered her spectacles and gave her guest a long look.

"But Viper," she said, "these aren't wishes. They're regrets."

"What's the difference?" Viper said. "Goodnight, Nica."

*   *   *

The Viper stepped out into the bone-chilling damp of the Weehawken night. A patrol car was parked at the curb. A uniformed driver sat behind the wheel. Detective Red Carney was standing on the sidewalk, waiting for the Viper. If Viper was going to shoot Carney, now was the moment. He could then kill the other cop and escape in the patrol car.

"Good evening, Viper," Carney said.

"Hello, Red."

"Well, I just came from the hospital. Yolanda is awake and alert. She confessed."

"Confessed?"

"To the murder of Randall 'Country' Johnson. She says he tried to rape her. She stabbed him in self-defense. Seems like an open-and-shut case to me."

"Jesus Christ."

"You're one lucky son of a bitch, Viper. Now get in the car. I'll drive you to the hospital to see Yolanda."

Yo-Yo was sitting up in the bed when Viper entered her Harlem Hospital room. Viper had never seen her look quite like this: utterly drained, haunted.

"Hello, Clyde."

"How are you, Yo-Yo?"

"Physically, I'm all right . . ."

"But you're sick in your soul, is that what you want to say?"

"I don't know what's wrong with me, Clyde."

"Neither do I."

"Red Carney says I won't be charged. I'm a free woman."

"Thank you, Yo-Yo. You might have saved my life tonight."

"Well, I owed you, Clyde."

"So what now?"

"Well . . ." Yolanda gave a wan smile. Viper saw a flicker of her usual radiance. "We recorded a great album, didn't we?"

"Yes, we did."

"We can do more. Please don't give up on me, Clyde. Please. Will you give me one more chance? Just one more chance?"

The Viper stared hard into Yolanda's eyes. He didn't know what to say.

AUTHOR'S PLAYLIST

T HIS NOVEL IS steeped in the history and the mythol-
ogy of jazz. For more than forty years, I've always
listened to music while I write. Here are fifty of the tracks
I listened to most while working on this novel.

"'Round Midnight": performed by Thelonious
Monk, original 1948 recording
"'Round Midnight": performed by the Miles Davis
Quintet, 1957 recording
"Viper's Dream": performed by Django Reinhardt
"Stardust": performed by Louis Armstrong
"West End Blues": performed by Louis Armstrong
"St. Louis Blues": performed by Louis Armstrong
"The Man I Love": performed by Billie Holiday
"Strange Fruit": performed by Billie Holiday
"Strange Fruit": performed by Nina Simone
"Moten Swing": performed by Bennie Moten's
Kansas City Orchestra
"Jumpin' at the Woodside": performed by Count
Basie and His Orchestra

"Lester Leaps In": performed by Count Basie's Kansas City Seven with Lester Young on saxophone

"Draftin' Blues": performed by Count Basie and His Orchestra

"If You're a Viper": performed by Fats Waller

"Sing Sing Sing": performed by Benny Goodman and His Orchestra

"Body and Soul": performed by Coleman Hawkins

"Take the A Train": performed by Ella Fitzgerald

"The Mooche": performed by Duke Ellington and His Orchestra

"Caravan": performed by Duke Ellington and His Orchestra

"Jungle Nights in Harlem": performed by Duke Ellington and His Orchestra

"Prelude to a Kiss": performed by Duke Ellington and His Orchestra

"Such Sweet Thunder": performed by Duke Ellington and His Orchestra

"In the Mood": performed by Glenn Miller and His Orchestra

"Ko-Ko": performed by Charlie Parker's Reboppers

"Now's the Time": performed by Charlie Parker's Reboppers

"Night in Tunisia": performed by the Charlie Parker Septet

"Parker's Mood": performed by Charlie Parker's All Stars

"Lover Man": performed by the Charlie Parker Quintet

"Salt Peanuts": performed by Dizzy Gillespie and
   His All-Star Quintet

"Manteca": performed by Dizzy Gillespie and His
   Orchestra

"Dance of the Infidels": performed by Bud
   Powell

"Nica's Dream": performed by Art Blakey and the
   Jazz Messengers

"Rhythm in a Riff": performed by Billy Eckstine
   and His Orchestra

"My One and Only Love": performed by Art
   Tatum and Ben Webster

"Si Tu Vois Ma Mère": performed by Sidney
   Bechet

"April in Paris": performed by Sarah Vaughan

"So What": performed by Miles Davis

"Naima": performed by John Coltrane

"St. Thomas": performed by Sonny Rollins

"Django": performed by the Modern Jazz
   Quartet

"Take Five": performed by the Dave Brubeck
   Quartet

"Lonely Woman": performed by Ornette
   Coleman

"Goodbye Pork Pie Hat": performed by Charles
   Mingus

"The Black and Crazy Blues": performed by Rahsaan Roland Kirk

"The Inflated Tear": performed by Rahsaan
   Roland Kirk

"Green Onions": performed by Booker T. and the
   M.G.'s

"In a Sentimental Mood": performed by Duke
    Ellington and John Coltrane
"In Walked Bud": performed by Thelonious Monk
"Pannonica": performed by Thelonious Monk
"Crepuscule with Nellie": performed by Theloni-
    ous Monk

ACKNOWLEDGMENTS

I WOULD LIKE TO thank my colleagues and comrades-in-arts in France, most especially my two champions at Rivages Noir: François Guérif and Jeanne Guyon. *Merci infiniment!*